Trumpula

A Novel

Greg Mandel

authorHOUSE®

AuthorHouse™
1663 Liberty Drive
Bloomington, IN 47403
www.authorhouse.com
Phone: 1 (800) 839-8640

Published by AuthorHouse 09/23/2017

ISBN: 978-1-5462-1018-4 (sc)
ISBN: 978-1-5462-1017-7 (e)

Library of Congress Control Number: 2017914819

Print information available on the last page.

For
My mother, Frances,
and for immigrants everywhere

THE NOTES OF DONALD J. TRUMPULA AS RECORDED ON OBAMA'S SECRET WIRETAPP SURVEILLANCE SYSTEM

9th January, 2017 – Hello, Barack. It's me, The Donald, 45th President of the United States. As you know, I won the election with a massive landslide victory in the Electoral College. Yuge landslide, tremendous, greatest landslide in the history of landslides. I had election night, 306. So I'm sitting here in my precious Trumpula Tower, and I know you're listening, surveilling me on your secret wiretapp, which you've hidden inside my electric toothbrush or blender or wherever you put it. Kellyanne thinks it's in the microwave. I checked this morning when I was reheating my KFC, but I couldn't find anything. You're a bad, sick guy, Barack. I'll find it, believe me. I get great intel. Really terrific intel. The best. We're looking into it very, very strongly. At a certain point in time I'll be revealing some interesting things, and I think people will be extremely impressed.

I'm sure being President will be a piece of cake. The most beautiful piece of cake you've ever seen. Very, very easy. If you could do it, Barack, you, who wasn't even born in this country, how hard can it be for someone with my amazing, very good brain? Anyway, in my spare time, I've decided to write a new book, because all my books are totally amazing, they have all the best words, and they sell millions of copies. I'm probably the bigliest-selling author in the history of books, okay? I went to an Ivy League school, I'm very yugely educated. I know words, I have all the best words. I have the best, but this one's going to be different. It'll be a memoir of my tremendous, historical life. I'm going to call it: "Interview With a Vampire President." What's that, Kush? My Senior Adviser, Jared Kushner, the luckiest man on the face of the earth because he happens to be married to my beautiful, voluptuous, sexy daughter-bride, Ivanka, tells me that this title has already been stolen from me by this nasty woman, Anne Rice. See you in court, Anne! Okay, fine. If I can't use that title I'll call it "Bite Me: Donald J. Trumpula's Life as the Greatest Vampire President Ever in the History of the Universe. PERIOD!" By Count Donald J. Trumpula.

Chapter One: How The Bigliest Story Ever Told Began. I was sitting in a Turkish bath in my hometown of Kallstadt, Germany, minding my own business, bathing my luxurious Mango Tango skin in the soothing heat of the amazingly opulent thermal bath waters. The year was 1686. Of course, at that time, my name was spelled differently. I was Donald J for Johann Drumpfula, with a D. And I was in the bath, very terrific, exclusive Turkish bath with great, high-end clientele, and suddenly I felt a strange, pricking sensation on my neck, like I was pricked by some small pricking thing that pricks other things. And I turned around and there, through the thick, billowing steam, I saw the most strikingly handsome, shirtless vampire in probably the history of shirtless vampires, okay? He was a Russian, and he had the most piercing Maximum Blue eyes you've ever seen, I'll never forget, and he introduced himself to me as Vladimir "The Impaler" Poutine. And he's the one who originally got me started in the vampire business.

We became great, great friends, Vlad and I, though I don't know him, we've never met, don't have a relationship, because what's a relationship? And we remain so to this day. I learned a lot about biting from Vlad – although I also think biting is a natural trait. Sucking too, but they're two different things, okay? You either have it or you don't, biting. You get better at it, learning certain techniques and so forth, where to puncture the neck and things of that nature, it's very technical. The people that I know who are great biters or great blood suckers or great at cape twirling or turning into bats, it's very natural, very natural. Like dunking a basketball or being a good golfer. And luckily I'm a natural at all of those, believe me. The most natural you've ever seen, okay?

So anyway, Vlad got me started in the vampire business, made me immortal, so I'll never get old, as you can tell just by looking at me. I mean, I'm still very, very, very handsome, and in perfect shape with my six-pack abs and perfect glutes. I can tell every time I watch the luscious Burnt Sienna skin folds of my backfat as I flex and practice my golf swing naked in front of one of my many full-length mirrors. Not that I can see anything, because I cast no reflection, but I can hear the amazing muscles of my torso as they ripple. If you're wondering how I remain so tremendously handsome and in shape, with the body and skin of a much younger man, it's because… I'm a vampire. Did I mention that? And also because I kidnapped Richard Simmons and I keep him in a giant hole in the dungeon of my luxurious castle here in Manhattan, Trumpula Tower, so that I have access to his incredibly amazing exercise theories 24/7. [shouting] IT PUTS THE SPRAY TAN IN THE BASKET, RICHARD! [Back to normal voice] Smart people, that Richard Simmons. We share the same beautiful Neon Carrot skin tone, as well as a deep and abiding love of sweating to the oldies.

As you know I'm currently married to Melania, and she's great, but getting up there, let's face it. She's, what, 40 now? 45? So, it's checkout time for me. Once they hit 35 it's checkout time, believe me. And I found this new girl, when I was in Washington, and she really, really blew me away, because she's a perfect double for this girl I used to know two, three hundred years ago. She was my soulmate, my one true love, the love of my life, the one who got away. Her name was… I forget her name, it's been so long, but I was deeply in lust with this girl. She was married, but I moved on her very, very heavily. In fact, I took her out furniture shopping. She wanted to get some nice furniture. I said, 'I'll show you where they have some nice furniture.' And then I grabbed her by the pussy – or, as we called it in those days, the crinkum crankum – and just started kissing, even though I didn't have any Tic Tacs, because Tic Tacs hadn't been invented yet. And, well, it ended badly because I'm a vampire so I divested her of all of her blood and she died. It's called *winning*, okay? But there was something about her I never forgot. I went to her funeral, you know, after I divested her and it was very, very sad, but very, very, very beautiful. Very, very beautiful. Her family was there. Incredible family, loved her so much. So devastated, they were so devastated. But the ceremony was amazing. They served the greatest food, the most beautiful jumbo shrimp balls you've ever seen. So amazing. The best. And now, this new girl, I saw her the other day in downtown Washington and I said, 'Who the hell is THAT? She looks just like what's her name, my soulmate, from centuries ago.' I found out she works in a library in Washington, downtown. So I had my people get her information, and I'm gonna move on her like a bitch. I'll take her back to my amazingly opulent castle and make her part of my harem. Like Procol Harum. A whiter shade of pale, which perfectly describes not only my brides but everyone who voted for me. She's a 9, yeah, solid 9. Currently dating this no-talent loser, but I've got a plan. The best plan ever, believe me.

PART ONE

MAR-A-LAGO

JONATHAN HARKER'S E-MAIL

13th January, 2017; 11:06 p.m.
To: Mimi
From: Jonathan
Subject: Arrival

Dear Mimi, I've arrived in Palm Beach, which seems like a really cool place (not really – it's quite warm, actually!) from the glimpse I got of it in the dark out the windows of the plane as we were landing. With all the palm trees lining the streets, it feels like the tropics, like a private island in the Caribbean maybe, belonging to some corrupt generalissimo. If Chile is the "delicate waist of the Americas," as Neruda wrote, what does that make Florida, but a jutting, beak-like nose drooping from the giant, swollen head that is the rest of our country?

As I deplaned, I heard my name called from the loudspeaker, directing me to the white courtesy telephone. I picked it up, and an officious-sounding female voice directed me to the Information counter. When I got there, I found a small, very delicate-looking woman, dark-complexioned and with long, black hair, tied up quite neatly in a colorful green scarf. She looked like a gypsy, like a younger version of Maria Ouspenskaya, that actress from the old Wolfman films. She wore a flowing red-and-white dress, which had affixed to its breast a nametag that read: "Katina." To complete the ensemble, she spoke with a sharp Eastern European accent.

"You are the real estate lawyer?" she said. "From Washington? Jonathan Harker?"

"Yes," I said, a bit bumfuzzled at her prescience. "I am."

She smiled and whispered something to a young, pale-skinned man in white shirt-sleeves, who stood beside her behind the counter. He turned away to retrieve something from a desk behind them, and returned with a small, gold-leafed envelope with my name scrawled in ornate letters in thick, blood-red ink across its back. I tore it open and read the card:

Mr. Harker –

Welcome to Florida. I am anxiously expecting you. My private limousine will bring you to me. I trust that your journey from the horrible, burning, crime-infested inner city hellscape of Democrat-controlled Washington, D.C. – which is more dangerous than Afghanistan and Iraq put together times 1000 – has been a happy one, if you were lucky enough to make it to the airport without getting shot. I'm sure that you will enjoy your stay in my beautiful, luxurious Mar-a-Lago, which is the greatest estate in the history of the universe. We have a lot of work to do to finish this deal. I hope you are up to it, as you come highly recommended by Mr. Hawkins. You'd better be, or you're fired.

– Trumpula

I asked Katina if she had ever met my client, the Count, and could tell me anything of his resort palace, Mar-a-Lago. She and her pale-skinned underling looked at each other in a frightened sort of way and, crossing themselves, said that they knew nothing, then went silent, simply refusing to speak further. It was all very mysterious and a bit unsettling. You would think the people here would be more than happy to acknowledge the presence of the President-Elect.

I picked up my bags and turned to leave, but Katina came out from behind the counter and grabbed my arm.

"Must you go? Oh, young Mr. Harker, must you go?" She was in such a state that she seemed to have lost her grip as a professional dispenser of airport information.

When I told her that yes, I had to go, and that I was engaged on important real estate business, she asked: "Do you know what day it is?"

I answered that of course I knew what day it was, it was Friday.

She shook her head in a flustered sort of manner, and said, "Oh, yes! I know that, I know that! But do you know what *day* it is?"

When I told her I didn't understand, she went on: "It is Friday the 13th, the eve of Saint Hugo's Day. Do you not know that tonight, when the clock strikes midnight, just a little over an hour from now, all the evil things in the world will have full sway? Do you know where you are going, and what you are going to?" She was in such distress that I tried to comfort her, but without success. Finally she dropped to her knees and implored me not to go; at least to wait a day or two before starting. It was all very ridiculous, but I don't mind telling you, Mimi, it made me feel very uncomfortable. I helped her up, and said that I thanked her, but that I represented the firm of Hawkins & Co., and I was expected at the palace of Count Donald J. Trumpula – the newly-elected President of the United States—to conduct some important real estate business. She then rose and dried her eyes, and, taking a crucifix from around her neck, offered it to me. I didn't know how to react, because, being an agnostic, as you know, I regard such things as, well, sort of foolish, and yet it seemed so ungracious to refuse the lady who seemed so well-meaning. She put the rosary 'round my neck and said, "For your mother's sake," then returned to her place behind the Information counter.

I am now sitting on a bench beneath a tall, ornate street lamp outside the Baggage Claim area, writing you this email on my phone while I wait for the Count's limousine, which is, of course, late; this place is very warm for January, even now at 11 o'clock at night, and the crucifix is still 'round my neck. Whether it is the gypsy woman's fear, or the heat of this place, or the crucifix itself, I don't know, but I'm perspiring through my shirtsleeves, and not feeling nearly as relaxed as I was on the flight down here. Ah, finally, here's the limo!

JONATHAN HARKER'S E-MAIL

14th January, 2017; 12:39 a.m.
To: Mimi
From: Jonathan
Subject: The Client

A very long, black limousine with impenetrably black windows pulled up without a sound in front of the bench where I sat. The driver exited the limo. He appeared to be an albino, pale as the angel of death, tall and broad-shouldered, dressed all in black, with very white, perfectly coiffed Aryan hair beneath his black chauffeur's cap, a square jaw, and a steely glare that he fixed directly upon me as he walked around the car, strong, muscled arms swinging stiffly at his sides. I recognized him immediately. It was Mike Pence. He did not smile, and the lamplight fell on a hard-looking mouth, with very pale, thin, lips and sharp-looking teeth, as white as ivory. He stopped a few feet away from where I sat, squinting angrily at me. "Mr. Harker?" His voice was an echo that seemed to come from some hollow place deep inside him.

"Yes," I said, rising to my feet. I took a step towards him, but he put up a large, pink palm.

"Before you come any closer," he said, "I need to ask you a question."

I stopped in my tracks. "What's that?"

He gritted his gleaming, white teeth, pink eyes pinched into angry slits, his facial muscles twitching into a twisted grimace. Finally, he spoke. "Are you... a homosexual?" He looked as if just saying the word caused him physical pain.

"Uhh, no," I said, glancing around, looking to see if anyone else had heard what the Vice President-Elect had just asked me. "Why do you ask?"

Mike Pence seemed to relax his facial muscles just a bit, and he let out a soft breath of relief. "Because if you were, I'd have to call for another driver. But you're not, so it's okay."

Without a word he moved briskly toward me, then bent

over and swept my bags up in one effortless motion. Then turning, he opened the rear door of the limo and held it open, still squinting sullenly at me while I climbed inside. As I settled onto the cold, leather seat cushions, he slammed the door, then put my bags in the trunk and slammed that, too, before getting back behind the wheel. He put the limo in gear and we took off, sweeping along the highway in near complete silence. For the next fifteen minutes we swooped quietly through the dark night, until a soft buzzing sound cut the silence. I watched the glass partition between the driver's seat and the back of the limo descend smoothly, removing the barrier between myself and Mike Pence. I could see his steely eyes squinting at me in the rear view mirror.

"Mr. Harker," he said in a low, barely-contained growl.

"Yes?" I responded.

"You don't have any other... persons... joining you at a later time, is that correct?"

I shook my head. "No." Again I added: "Why do you ask?"

"Because," he said through tightly-clenched teeth. "If you did, and she was a female, I would be forced to call for another driver."

Now it was me doing the squinting, as I tried to guess what his purpose was in telling me this. "Why is that?" I asked.

"Because," he said. "I can not be alone with a woman who is not Mother."

I was afraid to ask, but I simply had to. "You – you can't be alone with a woman who isn't your mother?"

"Not my mother," he said. "Mother. My wife."

TRUMPULA

"I see." There followed an awkward silence, until I decided to break it. "Congratulations on the election."

He said nothing, so I tried again. "How do you like working for Count Trumpula? Must be... exciting?"

"I don't know anything," he said tightly. "I don't hear anything. I don't see anything. I don't smell anything. Whatever you've been told that I heard, saw, or smelled is incorrect."

I opened my mouth to speak, but couldn't think of what to say, and before I could come up with another question, he pushed a button and the glass divider whirred efficiently back up between us, returning us to our separate silences.

"Okay," I said to the empty seat facing me. I turned toward the window and watched the moon appear from behind a dark cloud as we turned down a long, palm-lined drive that led to the front gate of Mar-a-Lago, a gleaming, gold-leafed arch whose gilded doors swung open seemingly automatically at our approach. We drove through the golden entrance and pulled into the courtyard of a vast, sprawling palace, from whose tall, dark windows no light shone.

When the limo stopped, Mike Pence got out, and immediately my door was flung open. Scarcely had I exited the back seat before Mike Pence slammed the trunk closed, then strode forcefully and silently past me, still squinting fiercely as he climbed back behind the wheel and slammed the driver's door shut. Then, with a roar, the limo swooped away into the night, leaving me standing alone at the entrance to the palace, my bags behind me. I picked them up and walked the few steps to the palace's great door, which must have been ten feet tall, and seemed very old, built of thick oak and studded with large, iron nails. It

7

appeared to have been constructed to withstand a tank, or, at the very least, a battering ram. I stood there in silence, not knowing what to do. There was no sign of any bell or knocker. I began to wonder what sort of place I had come to, and to what kind of people? What sort of crazy errand has old man Hawkins sent me on, I thought? Is this some kind of initiation or hazing for the newly minted lawyer? Do all the new associates get sent down here to this place after just passing the bar?

I began to rub my eyes and pinch myself to see if I was dreaming, half expecting to suddenly awake and find myself back home, lying next to you, sweet Mimi, in our bed, with the D.C. dawn streaming in through the windows of our apartment on K Street. But no such luck! My eyes were not deceiving me. I was indeed awake and among the Floridians.

Just as I had sold myself on this fact, I heard a heavy step approaching from behind the great door. There was the sound of rattling chains and the clanking of a massive bolt being drawn back, and the great door swung open.

Within stood a bloated, orange-faced man, clean-shaven, and dressed in a flowing robe of black and purple silks, with a black cape draped across his shoulders and back. Lapis lazuli eyes, small and narrow, as blue as the cool, cerulean waters of the Pacific, stared unblinking at me, beautiful and serene, yet somehow I couldn't shake the feeling that those eyes were as empty and soulless as the cold, lifeless eyes of the great white shark. On top of his head was a swirly brass-blond mane of cotton-candy hair, whooshing over his forehead in a gravity-defying swoop, held in place by enough hairspray to blow a hole in ten ozones. I stared, completely transfixed. Why, I'm sure I couldn't tell you; it was just hair, after all. And yet I felt myself strangely mesmerized by this hair; it seemed to hold some unnatural power and, for lack of a better word, danger.

The man motioned me in with a courtly gesture, waving the stubby, delicately manicured fingers of his unnaturally small, pink hand. He pursed his bloodless lips and said in excellent English, but with a strange intonation, "Welcome to my incredibly beautiful home. It's so beautiful you wouldn't believe it. Enter freely and of your own will!" He stood like a statue, as though his invitation had turned him to stone. The instant, however, that I stepped over the threshold, he suddenly darted forward, and holding out his tiny hand, grasped mine with the determined grip of an angry child, a child with the clenching power of a giant gorilla! Besides his vice-like grip, his hand was as cold as ice – more like the hand of a dead corpse than a living man.

He bowed in a courtly way as he said, "I am Trumpula, and I bid you welcome, Mr. Harker, to Mar-a-Lago, my vast and opulent estate. Unfortunately, it is late, and my servants have all gone to bed. Sad."

With that, my odd host lifted my bags as if they were made of nothing more than paper and, turning, seemed to glide up the great, winding staircase, then along a long passageway, his feet not visible or making any sound as he moved, even though my own steps rang heavily on the stone floor as I followed him. At the end of this passageway, he threw open a heavy door, and I was happy to see a well-lit room with a large, four-poster bed that looked quite inviting. The Count set my luggage on the floor, just inside the doorway.

"I trust you will be comfortable here," he said, ushering me inside. As I walked past him into the chamber, I felt his tiny, pink hands graze along my shoulder blades, and I could not repress a shudder. My host, evidently noticing my revulsion, drew back, and produced a grim sort of smile, revealing two fangs, sharp and deadly looking on either side of a set of shiny white teeth.

Worried that I might have offended him, I smiled back. "Thank you, Count Trumpula," I said.

His grin widened, but there was nothing happy in it. It was like the grin of a wolf spying a defenseless little rabbit. He pursed his lips in that strange way he did before speaking. "You may call me... The Donald." Suddenly, through the open window across the room, there came the sound of loud hooting, howling and grunting, like a pack of wild jungle apes. It sent a cold shiver up my spine, but The Donald's eyes gleamed, and he said, "Listen to them – the children of the night. What music they make! The best music, terrific."

I swear, Mimi, I felt the hair stand up on the back of my neck. "I didn't know you had monkeys in Florida," I said to him.

"Not monkeys," said the Count. "Orangutans. Bigly ones. Yuge. The best orangutans you'll find anywhere on the planet. There are many things here which you may find surprising, Mr. Harker. I would advise that you keep to your room after dark. Mar-a-Lago can be a treacherous place at night." Suddenly he cast a furtive glance over his shoulder, as if looking for some hidden enemy lurking in the shadows. Then he scuttled close to me, so close I could smell the foulness of his fetid breath. It smelled like carrion. "Beware! Take care!" he hissed in a whisper, his eyes narrowing to red, beady slits and darting this way and that. "Obama has wire-tapped this whole place! He may be here even now, watching us from under the bed, or hiding in the closet! He's a bad – or sick – guy!" I expected him to burst into laughter at his little joke, but he didn't, and, with a sick feeling in the pit of my stomach, I realized he was deathly serious. Suddenly he let go of my hand and glided across the room to a small side table, where a bottle of vodka stood next to a pair of crystal tumblers. "Would you care for a drink? T&T, perhaps? Trump and Tonic. My own label. Trump Vodka. You remember, I'm sure. It was the best, Harker. Everything I do is the best."

I remembered reading somewhere about his vodka venture. He'd predicted the T&T would become one of the most requested drinks in America, but then the vodka went bust, like so many of his schemes.

"Are you having one?" I asked.

"Oh no," he said. "I never drink…. alcohol."

"Then I'll pass," I said. "I'm afraid I'm not a vodka man, anyway."

A tiny, bubbling pool of spittle the color of edelweiss appeared at the corner of his mouth, and a faint hissing sound came from his small, round mouth. He glided past me to the door, and again I felt a chill as he went past. He started to leave, closing the door halfway before he stopped, and, turning to me, said: "Tomorrow you shall sleep as late as you wish. I have to be away till the afternoon, but when I return we will talk business, and I will make your firm millions of dollars, Mr. Harker. You'll make so many dollars you're going to beg me to stop making you dollars. So sleep well, and dream well." And with a courteous bow, he left, closing the door behind him. As soon as he was gone, the temperature in the bedroom seemed to rise noticeably. Again, I shivered, and strange thoughts raced through my mind.

MIMI MURRAY'S E-MAIL

14th January, 2017; 12:52 a.m.
To: Jonathan
From: Mimi
Subject: The Client

Hello my One True Love, so glad to hear you've arrived safe and sound in sunny FLA. I loved reading your email – you have the soul of a poet, my dear—but crap on a Frappucino, that is one crazy story about the gypsy woman! And the Count – you make him sound like Bela Lugosi on shrooms! I know Count Cheeto's the King of the Weirdos, but it sounds like there might be something more than just your average, everyday, run-of-the-mill Tea Party dipshittery, moral bankruptcy and raging, full-throated racism going on down there, like maybe there's something behind all that Trumpula's-a-Vampire talk, huh? Do ya think?

Hitting the hay now. Kung Fu class was ridiculous today. We practiced our roundhouse kicks, and Patience and Fortitude are worn out after kicking so much butt! That's what I've named my newly weaponized feet, by the way, after the famous lions sitting outside the New York Public Library. Don't fuck with Patience and Fortitude! □

Anyhoo, good night, keep me posted, and, above all, stay safe, my love. I miss you already! Talk soon.

XOXO

—M

COUNT TRUMPULA'S TWITTER ACCOUNT

Donald J. Trumpula@RealTrumpula 14th January, 2017, 1:01 a.m.

J. Harker from DC, a smart person with a very nice neck. Not like Chris Christie, whose neck is fat & disgusting! The worst. #Loserblood

Donald J. Trumpula@RealTrumpula 14th January, 2017, 1:03 a.m.

Wrong. Christie's is not the worst neck. McConnell's is the worst. There's no blood in there! I think he's already undead. #chickenneck

Donald J. Trumpula@RealTrumpula 14th January, 2017, 1:04 a.m.

I was right the first time. It's Christie. #toomanychins

JONATHAN HARKER'S E-MAIL

14th January, 2017; 11:13 p.m.
To: Mimi
From: Jonathan
Subject: The Client

Dear Mimi,

Last night I slept fitfully, strange dreams permeating my sleep. Throughout the night I could hear the Count's television, blaring away while he shuffled endlessly around the palace until dawn. I could hear him changing the channel from one cable news network to the next, with the occasional enraged outburst of "Fake news!" or "Liberal media!"

My room was very warm, with no breeze to speak of, even though I left the window open, but eventually I was able to drop off to sleep.

One dream, in particular, I recall. I was in my suite in Count Trumpula's palace where he has put me up, sleeping, as I was in reality, when suddenly I heard what sounded like the flapping of wings from just outside my window, growing closer and closer. In the dream, a dark shadow passed over my eyes, fluttering over me as I slept, the wings sounding as if they were buffeting directly above me. In my dream state, I opened my eyes to see a giant, black bat, hovering over me, its eyes glowing red as embers and seeming to stare straight at me with a strange menace. On its head was a weird tuft of blond hair, which reminded me quite a bit of the Count's. I wanted to call out, or strike at the creature, but I could not move, transfixed by its blood-red eyes and curious hair, which held me as if in a trance. The creature stayed there for some time, hovering, watching me, before suddenly its disgusting mouth yawned open, revealing its sharp, gleaming fangs. The bat let out a screech then, a sound that seemed to come from another world, and then it flitted off out the window. In my dream, I collapsed back into a fitful slumber.

It was well past noon when I finally awoke, sweaty and

agitated from the dark images that haunted my sleep. Good God, I thought, I'd slept the entire day away! I rose, and made my way to my suite's adjoining bathroom. Strangely, there was no mirror, but luckily I have the little antique shaving glass you gave me for Christmas, M, which I hung above the sink and was just beginning to shave when suddenly I felt a cold, babyish hand on my shoulder, and heard the Count's voice whispering to me, "Good afternoon." I started, turning toward him, for it amazed me that I had not seen him in the mirror. In starting, I cut myself slightly on my chin, and there was a thin line of blood trickling down my skin. When Trumpula saw it, his eyes blazed red with a sort of demonic fury, and he made a sudden grab at my face. Wiping the blood from my chin with his incredibly short fingers, he brought them to his lips, and, with a loud, slurping sound, sucked my blood from his fingertips.

Not believing my eyes, I turned back to the mirror to see how I could have missed him, but somehow he wasn't there again, though clearly he was, for the man *was* there, close to me, I could actually see him out of the corner of my eye! But there was no reflection of him in the mirror. Nothing! It was all so very queer and unsettling.

"Excuse me," I said. "Did you just… drink my blood?"

"No," he said. "Fake news!" as he finished sucking my blood from his stubby cocktail-weiner fingers. And then he withdrew from the room without uttering another word.

When I finished shaving, and showering, I emerged from my rooms and made my way down that dark hallway outside my door. I could see no one, but could hear what sounded like the clinking of silverware coming from a room downstairs, so I made my way down, and followed the sounds to the dining room. When I entered, I found The Count sitting at a large table, with a gigantic bucket of Kentucky Fried Chicken before him. And, Mimi, he was cutting up a drumstick with a knife and fork. He smiled at me, and his lips ran back over his gums, showing the long, sharp, canine teeth I'd seen earlier. "Hello, Harker. Would you like to join me for breakfast?"

"It's a little late for breakfast, isn't it?" I responded.

"It's breakfast time, Harker. See? Nine a.m." He grinned wolfishly, and thrust his left wrist at me, revealing a garish, white gold and diamond-encrusted watch from his Trumpula Signature Collection. I could tell by the word TRUMPULA emblazoned in gold lettering across the white face, just below 12 o'clock.

I let out a small chuckle. "That's not right. Your watch has stopped." I showed the Count the time on my watch. "It's nearly two o'clock."

Trumpula frowned, his tiny azure eyes narrowing to hooded slits in his pumpkin-colored face. "Wrong! It's working very nicely. So nicely you wouldn't believe it. It's just displaying an alternative time, Harker. If you want to work with me on this deal, we'll need to be synchronized. Synchronize to nine a.m. Go ahead. Synchronize, Harker."

He stared at me until I changed my watch to nine a.m. Then I sat at the table across from him, and he passed me the giant bucket of chicken, from which I took a breast and a thigh. As I started to eat with my hands, the Count stopped me and insisted I use a knife and fork. What a very peculiar man!

I asked him about Mar-a-Lago, and where all of the club members were, and he explained to me that the club is separated by a very thick wall from his private residence in the palace. "It's a great wall, Harker, the best. Go ahead, scream your head off. No one can hear you. I have thick walls. Incredibly thick. Amazing. The best walls, believe me. And nobody builds walls better than me, trust me, and I build them very inexpensively. Just like the great, great wall I will build on our southern border and I will make Mexico pay for that wall. Because when Mexico sends their people, they're not sending the best. They're sending people that have lots of problems, and they're bringing their problems with them. They're bringing drugs, they're bringing crime. They're rapists. And some, I assume, are good people. But somebody's doing the raping, Harker. I mean, somebody's doing it. Who's doing the raping? Who's doing the raping, Harker?"

I told him I didn't know who was doing the raping, although, with all the stories in the press about the many women coming forward to accuse the Count of groping and trying to bite them, I think if I had to name one person who I thought might be doing the raping, it would probably be him.

Upon finishing our "breakfast," The Donald and I started the work he'd engaged the firm to complete – mainly, the purchase of a large estate called Carfax Abbey just outside of Washington. At one point, I inquired after his finances, asking him how he'd made his fortune. His reply was most strange. "Guano," he said, pursing his lips in that odd manner.

I stared at him, not certain I had heard correctly. "Did you say guano?"

"Yes. Guano." Now, you're probably thinking he was joking, Mimi, but his expression was utterly serious.

"And where do you get this… guano?" I asked. "Do you import it from Peru or Patagonia?"

"I make it myself," he said. "It's the best guano on the planet. The highest quality guano, amazing quality. So good you wouldn't believe it."

"You make it," I said, aware that I sounded like an echo. "You mean, you have a factory or manufacturing plant somewhere?"

"I have a process that I use to produce it, personally."

"A process?

"Amazing process," he said. "Unbelievable. Fantastic, beautiful process. Truly incredible. The best."

When I asked him what his market was for this guano, he informed me that he sells it to the Russians. "They love my guano, the Russians," he said. "They pay me a fortune for it. I also made a lot of money with Gaddafi. He came to the country, and he had to make a deal with me, because he needed the guano to fertilize his crops. Wheat crops, corn, falafel, I don't know. Crops. He paid me a fortune. Never got my guano. It became a sort of a big joke. He paid me more than I get from the Russians. And then, eh, didn't let him have any guano. I don't like to use the word screwed, but I screwed him. That's called being intelligent."

He then told me he wanted the firm – and myself, specifically – to explore China as a market for his guano. He thinks it could be quite lucrative, and that the firm could make a lot of money from the deal. I felt things were going quite smoothly, and he seemed to take quite an interest in me, personally, and my affairs. At one point he caught me looking at your photo on my phone, and he seemed to gasp. He asked me who it was, and I told him it was my fiancée. He seemed quite interested, and asked if he might have a closer look, so I gave him my phone and he held it for quite a long time, looking at your picture, M. He called you beautiful, a "solid 9 1/2," he said! "You're a very lucky man, Mr. Harker. Your fiancée is the epitome of feminine beauty."

I must have chuckled a bit, I guess, knowing how you would have reacted to that statement, and he asked me what was so funny. So I told him about you – he really was quite captivated. I told him that you're really quite the tomboy. How you do Kung Fu and all those other non-"ladylike" things you're so good at, how you can pummel any man I know, and yet, at the same time, be so completely feminine, vulnerable, and lovely. And how I love you even more because of it. He seemed completely transfixed, and did not want me to stop talking about you. In fact, he kept asking me questions about you, Mimi, until it actually started to feel a bit creepy, and when I tried changing the subject, and pointed out that we had much work yet to do, and then requested to see his taxes, he became suddenly irate, leaped from his seat and stormed from the room, slamming the door behind him. I waited nearly half an hour for him to come back, but he did not return.

Eventually, I gave up waiting and went on an exploration of the palace. I went up the stairs and looked out the window, admiring the view of the ocean, which was magnificent! But when I explored the palace further, I found that every door I came to was locked and bolted. In no place, save for the windows in the palace walls, is there even an exit! This can't be up to code. What if there's a fire? I'm beginning to feel as if Mar-a-Lago is a veritable prison, and I am a prisoner!

MIMI MURRAY'S E-MAIL

14th January, 2017; 11:37 p.m.
To: Jonathan
From: Mimi
Subject: The Client

OMG, Johnny! A prisoner? Really? Good one! And that bit about the KFC! And the "alternative time"—High-larious!

But, seriously, what's going on? I know how excited you are to be in Mar-a-Lago, working with Orange Hitler. You heard the news, right? There are going to be official investigations into the Trumpula-Vampire story! And also, he's going to give Steve Bannon a seat on the National Security Council. The guy from Breitbart? Zero national security experience? Flaming racist turd? Yeah, that guy. Speaking of turds... guano? For real? So gross! Are you sure this job is worth putting up with Count Kumquat? Lucy says that one of her suitors, Dr. Seward (I told you about him, he's the clinical psychologist from England) thinks Count T is actually suffering from some type of mental disease. He says he displays all the classic signs of malignant narcissism, and that he's dangerously mentally ill. Totally batshit. Ha! Get it? Batshit? Guano? Your little Mimi made a joke. ☺

Anyway, watch yourself, my dear! Miss you terribly!

Hurry up and finish your work so you can come home to me.

Sigh.

—M

COUNT TRUMPULA'S TWITTER ACCOUNT

Donald J. Trumpula@RealTrumpula 15th January, 2017, 1:36 a.m.

Vampire talk is a hoax put out by the Dems, and played up by the media, in order to mask the fact that Hairy Hillary is a werewolf!

Donald J. Trumpula@RealTrumpula 15th January, 2017, 1:38 a.m.

Why isn't the House Intelligence Committee looking into the Bill & Hillary deal that allowed Big Garlic to go to Transylvania? #MASA

JONATHAN HARKER'S E-MAIL

15th January, 2017; 2:36 a.m.
To: Mimi
From: Jonathan
Subject: The Client

Hey M. What a long, strange day it's been with the Count here at Mar-a-Lago. He was gone all day again, and I was left to my own devices. Where he goes, I have no idea, but I've yet to see him in daylight. Only at night.

Again, I slept fitfully, and didn't wake until nearly noon. After showering, I went downstairs and tried to go outside to look at the grounds, but the front door was locked from the outside. I couldn't get out, which only intensifies my feeling of being a prisoner in this place. I wandered around the palace, which seemed completely empty, trying to figure out how to get to the rest of the building, where the club is, and see what kind of people are willing to pay $200,000 in membership fees just to rub elbows with Trumpula! But every door I tried was locked, except one that led to the library. At least I think it is a library. There are vast shelves full of volumes, but at the same time the room is full of televisions! There are four of them, mounted on the walls. Giant flat screens, each tuned to a different news channel, but all muted, thank God! And the books, Mimi, they're all the same. Hundreds of copies of the Count's books. They were all there, and every one was autographed. *Trumpula: The Art of the Bite; Make it Count in Business and Life; Raising the Stakes: Trumpula's 10 Best Quotations On How To Make a Killing in Real Estate;* and *Time to Get Tough: Make America Suck Again.*

Sometime after sundown, the Count appeared, very anxious to get back to work. "Okay, Harker," he said. "So tell me about Washington and the amazing, tremendous estate you have purchased for me. It better be amazing and tremendous, Harker. I only live in very, very beautiful, luxurious places, trust me."

We went thoroughly into the business of the purchase of the estate at Carfax Abbey. I described it for him, how it fit his specifications perfectly. "It is on about 20 acres, and surrounded by thick woods," I told him, pulling some photos out of my briefcase. "The dense vegetation makes it a bit gloomy in spots. The house is very large, and quite old. There are only a few houses close by, the closest being a private lunatic asylum, which abuts the property on the east side of the estate. And, just as you requested, there is a swamp, just here."

He smiled thinly. "You know I'm going to drain it. Drain the swamp, Harker." He frowned a bit at the photos of the inside. "Those marble columns look old," he said. "And why would you use marble when you could use gold? Sad."

"If you don't mind me asking, Mr. Trumpula, why do you want to buy another estate in the Washington area? Obviously, you'll be living at the White House."

"To be perfectly honest, Mr. Harker," he said, "it's lust. The last time I was in Washington, I saw the most beautiful young girl. Very, very gorgeous. Total knockout. Not as voluptuous as Ivanka, because, as you know, if Ivanka weren't my daughter, perhaps I'd be dating her. But, no, I'd say this girl in Washington, she's a 10. Maybe a nine-and-a-half. Solid nine-and-a-half, yeah."

I was surprised to hear him talking about other women this way. Because he's married. "But what about your wife, Melania?" I asked him. "She's lovely."

He smiled, looking very sly and smug. And he sniffed loudly, as if he were coming down with a cold. "You've got a lot to learn, Harker," he said. "My wife, yeah, she's great. She's great. Beautiful. Still an 8. Maybe a 7-and-a-half. Used to be a 10. But she's sliding. She's 45, 46, whatever." He winced, moving his puffy, pink, pygmy mitts back and forth, as if he were playing an invisible accordion. "And, you know, it's time. Past time, because, what is it with women at 35, Harker? It's called 'checkout time.' 30 is the perfect age for a woman, but by the time they're 35, they've had too much life experience. 21 is nice, believe me, but it's embarrassing because they're still studying algebra. Now this girl, the one I'm after, she's about 24, 25 I'd say. Would I bang a 24-year-old? Oh, absolutely. I'd have no problem. I mean, I have an age limit, Harker. I don't want to be like Congressman Foley, with, you know, 12-year-olds. But I was looking at a girl the other day, had to be about 10 or 12, and I said to Billy Bush, you know, I'll be dating her in 10 years. Can you believe it?"

I was struck dumb, Mimi. I mean, truly speechless. It was disgusting. He's what? 70 years old, talking about dating young girls in their 20's? He's old enough to be their grandfather! And he's married! But he didn't even stop there. He just kept going, digging deeper, only pausing every five seconds or so to sniff through his nose like a cocaine fiend.

"I'm very attracted to beautiful girls, Harker. I just start kissing them. It's like a magnet. Just kiss. I don't even wait. And when you're a star they let you do it. You can do anything. Grab them by the pussy. That's what I'll do with this girl in Washington. Just grab her by the pussy. I don't know much about her. Not even her name, yet. *Sniff.* All I know is that she reminds me very much of a girl I used to know a long, long time ago. Ages ago, really. Seems like a couple of centuries, at least. And after all, how few days go to make up a century? She's a dead ringer for this girl I knew, Harker. Beautiful, stunning girl. Easy nine-and-a-half. Perfect in every way, almost. Maybe a little light up top. And this new girl, she's a perfect twin. And she's a librarian. Can you believe it? A bookworm. She works at the public library in D.C. Handing out free books to the poors and the blacks, who I have a very good relationship with. *Sniff.* She works at one of the downtown branches. I know that much. But I saw a photo of her and I knew I had to have her. *Sniff.*"

I felt my heart skip a beat. "A librarian, in Washington? Really. That's quite a coincidence. My fiancée, Mimi, is a librarian in Washington. At the Central Library, downtown. The Martin Luther King branch."

The Count grinned, and sniffed loudly two or three times. I thought I caught the beginnings of a smirk at the corners of his mouth, and in his eyes, and a cold feeling came over me as he spoke. "You don't say, Harker? Well, it's too bad you didn't bring her with you. She could be very useful to me, maybe."

I was quite flustered at the entire conversation. It made me feel dirty, talking to the Count about cheating on his wife, and with some girl at the library, Mimi. You probably know her, for God's sake! And by the expression on his stupid orange face, it seemed quite possible – even likely—that he knew *you* work at the library, and that is why he had Hawkins send me down here, to pick my brain. Or worse, your brain! I was disgusted by the whole thing, and wanted to get up and leave the place on the spot, damn the job! I could give a hang.

He continued talking about his "little bookworm," as he called her, this unsuspecting woman he has his sights set on.

"Of course, after next week, I'll be living in the White House full-time, more or less. So I'll be there. *Sniff.* But I'll need a little hideaway, Harker. A bachelor pad. Someplace I can take my little bookworm, you know, away from the inner city war zone, which is a total disaster."

He went on like this for hours, sniffing and babbling away about whatever topic seemed to pop into his head, jumping from subject to subject like a madman. This librarian in Washington, immigrants, Muslims, Obama loosening the lids on all his salt shakers – which he swears is a thing that happens—the "fake news," which is any media outlet that doesn't lick his boots, his guano deals with the Russians and now the Chinese – which he's very hot on. It was nearly 2 a.m. by the time we said goodnight. I must try and get some sleep now, darling Mimi. I will write more tomorrow, I promise.

MIMI MURRAY'S E-MAIL

15th January, 2017; 7:17 a.m.
To: Jonathan
From: Mimi
Subject: The Client

For the love of Benji, John! You HAVE to find out who this woman is! I need a name, so I can warn her! Count Creamsicle sounds like an absolute scumball on a personal level! I mean, everyone knows he's a total turdnado as a public figure. Like a sharknado, only with giant turds flying out of it. But he actually sounds worse in private, as a purported human being, if that's even possible. Jesus H. Christ on a jet-ski, can't you just leave? I'm sure if you explained to Old Man Hawkins he'd understand. Nobody should be forced to socialize with that fascist, baby-handed, serial groping Oompa Loompa. Not that you would ever ask to be taken off the job. You're so responsible! I love you. J

Heading to the library now. Talk later.

XOXO

—M

THE NOTES OF DONALD J. TRUMPULA AS RECORDED ON OBAMA'S SECRET WIRETAPP SURVEILLANCE SYSTEM

16th January, 2017 – Hello, Barack. It's me again, The Donald, 45th President of the United States. Continuing on with the recording of my book, "Bite Me: Donald J. Trumpula's Life as the Greatest Vampire President Ever in the History of the Universe. PERIOD!" by Count Donald J. Trumpula.

Chapter Two: The Bigliest Story Ever Told Continues. Now where was I? Oh yes, I just finished telling you about this woman back in the day who I moved on very heavily and ended up divesting her of all her blood and… she died. Terrible tragedy. But not all my relationships with women end badly. There was Marie Antoinette, very, very beautiful young woman, a solid 8. I met with her and her husband Louis in Versailles, which is great. It's great. Not as great as my Mar-a-Lago, but a decent palace. I give it a 7. Mar-a-Lago, of course, is a 10, as is my beautiful castle in New York, Trumpula Tower.

Anyway, the peasants were in revolt, very bad hombres, the peasants, paid agitators, probably paid by the Democrats. We were having dinner in Versailles, and we were still eating dessert. We had the most beautiful piece of cake you've ever seen. I mean, I don't know what cakes you've seen, Barack, but none of them could compare to this cake, believe me. And Marie was enjoying it, and we were given the message from the generals that the Assault on the Bastille was happening, and the garrison had opened fire, so the cannonballs were on the way, and I said, "Your Highness, let me explain something to you" – this is during dessert, and we've just fired 59 cannonballs, all of which hit, by the way... unbelievable... from you know, hundreds of feet away, all of which hit... amazing. It's so incredible, it's brilliant, it's genius. So what happens is I said, "Your Majesty, we've just launched 59 cannonballs heading toward the peasants." And we're almost finished with the dessert, and what does she do, Marie Antoinette? She offers this beautiful, amazing piece of cake, the most beautiful cake you've ever seen, to the peasants. She says, "Here, let them eat this incredible, amazing, beautiful piece of cake.' A really very, very beautiful gesture by a very classy lady.

But there was another woman I should tell you about. You may have heard of her. Her name was Pocahontas, and she was the daughter of an Indian chief, and she was truly, truly amazing. Very, very beautiful, very voluptuous, believe me. I give her a solid 8, yeah, solid 8. Maybe 8 ½. I met her in England, where she'd sailed with her husband, John Rolfe, from Jamestown. I met her at a masked ball, and I moved on her like a bitch. I moved on her and I failed, I'll admit it. She was married at the time to this loser, and I moved on her very, very heavily. In fact, I took her rug shopping. She wanted to get some nice rugs for her wigwam, or whatever, I don't know. I said, 'I'll show you where they have some nice rugs.' And then I grabbed her by the twaddle dandy—which is what we called it back in those days – and just started kissing. I kissed her very, very strongly, even though Tic Tacs still hadn't been invented. And then I bit her on the neck and sucked out all her blood, and… she died. A few years later I bought Manhattan from her father for a sack of marbles. Which is called winning, okay? This was after I'd come to America, but before the Revolutionary War. You do know I was in the Revolutionary War, don't you, Barack? Well, not *in* it, actually, because I got a deferment for my feet, but I'm the one who said the great, great, very famous line, "Give me liberty, or give me…" stop me if you've heard this before, Barack. When the British caught me at Chappaquiddich, I told them, "Give me liberty, or give me—fortune, and title, and land, and tax breaks, and more tax breaks, and more fortune because I blew the first one on some bad investments and puritan hookers. Or you can give me death. Wait, can we change that last part to a spanking? A light spanking, okay, because I bruise very easily. My Vivid Tangerine skin is very sensitive to lashing." That's what I told them. And guess what? They took the deal, and I went to work for the British as a spy. Very, very good deal for Trumpula.

Anyway, after that I went down to Florida, where I met a great, great man, Mr. Andrew Jackson, the greatest president ever until me, and we became great, great friends. Tremendous. We were business partners in this plantation. Had a lot of slaves. The best slaves. And I helped him relocate the Indians from Florida to their wonderful Genocide Centers in Oklahoma, where they later struck oil and became extremely wealthy. Very, very rich, believe me. We made the Indians so much money you wouldn't believe it, okay? And they were so happy. It was a great, great thing for them. Tremendous. They cried tears of joy all the way to Oklahoma, they were so happy. He had a yuge heart, Andrew Jackson. Yuge. He was a swashbuckler, and the Civil War made him so angry, so angry. We never would have had the Civil War if Andrew Jackson had been just a little later, we wouldn't have had it. Instead we got stuck with Lincoln, who is so overrated. People don't realize, you know, the Civil War, if you think about it, why? People don't ask that question, but why was there a Civil War? Why could that one not have been worked out? You know, maybe if Lincoln had been willing to compromise even a little. He could have said to the South, "Okay, here's what I'm going to do. You can have your slaves on Monday, Wednesday, and Friday. Tuesday and Thursday they get the day off. And every other weekend." I don't know, I'm just coming up with this off the top of my head, but I think it's pretty good. Something fair, like that. Why not?

But getting back to Andrew Jackson and his wife, a very, very attractive lady, believe me. I'd give her an eight and-a-half. I was there during that very mean and nasty campaign, helping out with the campaign, and I'll admit it, I moved on her very, very heavily, even though she was married. Still no Tic Tacs, but I grabbed her by the doodle sack – which is what we called it in those days—and just kissed. And then I bit her on the neck… and she died. Sad.

JONATHAN HARKER'S E-MAIL

16th January, 2017; 2:41 a.m.
To: Mimi
From: Jonathan
Subject: The Client

Dear Mimi, I again slept horribly. I think it must be the heat. This place is very warm at night, and there is no air conditioning in the palace. Also, the Count is up all night, shuffling around in his cape, watching Fox News, which he turns up very loud on his many televisions. It is nearly impossible to sleep, all I do is toss and turn, thinking about my conversations with the Count. Finally, sometime after four in the morning, I nodded off. Again, I dreamed of the giant bat with the goofy hair tuft, fluttering above my bed, watching me sleep with its creepy red eyes! I awoke just a few hours later, feeling as if I'd barely closed my eyes. After showering, I felt a bit better, and went to my door to leave, but I found it was locked from the outside! I pulled and pulled at the door, to no avail. I then took to banging on the door with my fists, and hollering at the top of my voice, but nobody came. I don't even know if there is anyone here besides myself and Count Trumpula, as I've yet to see another soul in the palace. No maids, no servants, no assistants. Nobody. Finally, after more than an hour of pounding and yelling for help, I gave up, as clearly no one can hear me. So, it's true, Mimi, I am a prisoner in this weird place! I thought of calling someone, but I don't know anyone here. And then I thought, I'll call 9-1-1. But how would that look? I'm a guest of the Count's, and he is my client – and an important client at that. What am I going to do, tell the police I've been kidnapped by the President-Elect? They'd haul me away to the booby hatch and throw away the key, and he'd drop the firm like a hot potato, old man Hawkins would be furious, and I'd be out of a job! No, I can't call the authorities. That was the thought process that went through my mind. Calming, I began to convince myself that it must just be some innocent mistake. An accident. My door must be jammed or something, and when the Count gets back from wherever it is he went, he will open the door and we'll have a good laugh over it. So I found some reading material in my bathroom – a couple of magazines left on a small table by the toilet – and sat myself down on the couch to read. But Mimi, when I looked at what the magazines were, a strange chill went through me. One is called "Coffin Beautiful," and the other, "Modern Vampire." And the articles, Mimi, they're all about the "vampire lifestyle," blood-sucking, and tips on where to find victims, and the best type of wood to use in your coffin, what kind of dirt to lay inside, and how to avoid religious symbols and counteract garlic! And the Count subscribes to these publications! Why? I know there are people out there who believe in vampires and actually think they are one of the "undead." Is Trumpula one of them???

Well, I read some, and paced the floor, thinking and waiting. I even thought about climbing out the window to try and make an escape, but it's simply too high and treacherous. My room is on the fourth floor, at least 40 feet up! I am stuck! A prisoner.

Finally, shortly after the sun went down, I heard a scratching at my door, and then the rattling of a key being fitted into the lock, and turning. And then the door pushed open, and there stood the Count. Well, I can tell you, I was quite steamed by this time, so I did not play nice. I asked him, "What's the meaning of this? Why am I locked in my room?"

He pursed his lips. "Because," he answered, like a petulant child.

"Because why?" I blurted out, getting angrier by the second.

"Because reasons," he said. "Many reasons. The best reasons. Many people have said so. Just ask them."

Well, how do you even respond to something like that? You can't. It's idiotic. Like arguing with a first-grader. Anyway, the Count was very keen to get back to work. He says he has a tight deadline to complete the purchase of the Washington property, and this guano deal, and honestly, I just want to finish it as well and get out of this awful place, so I went with him downstairs, where he had another bucket of KFC waiting. And we spent the entire night and into the early hours of the morning working straight through. We made very good progress, too, working until I was falling asleep on my feet. The Count then followed me up to my rooms, and bid me goodnight. After I closed the door, I heard him put the key in the lock and lock me in again! I am a prisoner, Mimi, of that there is no doubt!

MIMI MURRAY'S E-MAIL

16th January, 2017; 7:57 a.m.
To: Jonathan
From: Mimi
Subject: The Client

Oh, thank goodness you're okay, Johnny! I was really starting to worry, not hearing from you at all yesterday! God, I think you're right, you can't call the police. First of all, as you say, who would believe you? It's preposterous, the President-Elect a kidnapper? And yes, I agree, you would be putting your job in jeopardy. So you might not be able to call the police, but I could. Do you want me to? Do you even feel safe there? Should I get on a plane? I'll come down there and kick White Tang's ass if you want me to! Just say the word, okay? Patience and Fortitude shall be unleashed! ☐ Not that you need me to do your fighting for you. I do love how you stood up to him! He sounds completely horrid! And a terrible slave driver! Hurry and finish your business, and come home to me!

    Xoxo!!

Your devoted Mimi

p.s. Guess what we got to play with at Kung Fu class last night? Swords! Mr. Hirai says I'm a natural, and that I should get my own so I can practice outside of class, too. Lucy's absolutely green with envy!

COUNT TRUMPULA'S TWITTER ACCOUNT

Donald J. Trumpula@RealTrumpula 16th January, 2017, 7:14 p.m.

J. Harker is no hero. He's a LOOSER because he was captured! I don't like loosers. I like people that weren't captured, O.K.? #you'refired

JONATHAN HARKER'S E-MAIL

17th January, 2017; 4:51 a.m.
To: Mimi
From: Jonathan
Subject: Holy shit!

With all the strange goings-on last night, I couldn't sleep again, so, at about 12:30 I got up and went to the window. There was a full moon, and the courtyard beneath me was bathed in soft, yellow light, nearly as bright as daylight. As I leaned from my window, looking down, my eye was caught by something moving to my right, one floor below, which is where the Count has his rooms. I drew back and hid behind the curtain and looked out, watching. What I saw was astounding! It was Trumpula's head coming out from his window – no mistaking that strange, blond swoop of hair. At first I thought he must be just looking out at the moon, like me, but I knew I was wrong when I saw him slowly emerge from his window – his entire body! – and begin to crawl down the palace wall like a bug, *face down,* with his long, flowing cape spreading out around him like giant wings. At first I didn't believe my eyes. I thought it must be some trick of the moonlight, or some weird effect of shadow, but I kept watching (how could I not?), and there was no mistake. I could see his tiny little sausage fingers and toes grasping the stone walls of the palace, and he scuttled *down the wall* with speed, moving faster now, like some sort of lizard! He moved very quickly, at least 50 feet down, and then scuttled across just as far, before vanishing into a hole or window. I thought I must be losing my mind, Mimi, and no doubt that's probably what you're thinking right now, that I am going insane, but I swear to you it's true. It happened—I saw it with my own eyes!

Thinking I had to get out of that place, I took my phone and, using the flashlight app, went out of my room. Thankfully, my door was unlocked this time, but as I went down the pitch black hallway, trying all the other doors, they were all locked, as they had been earlier. I went down the long, stone staircase to the giant front door of the palace, where I had originally entered when I first came to this dreadful place, but it was still locked. I went all the way around the palace looking for another exit. I explored all the various stairs and corridors, all the downstairs windows – which all have bars on them, and I tried every door I came to. All locked! One or two small rooms near the hall were open, but there was nothing to see in them except old furniture, dusty with age and moth-eaten. At last I found one door at the end of a long, dim hallway in a separate wing of the palace I had not seen before. This door gave a little under pressure. I tried it again, and when I put my shoulder into it and pushed hard, it came open with a loud, creaking groan. I found myself in a dim room, along the south of the palace. The windows were curtainless, and the yellow moonlight flooded in through the diamond panes, softening the dust that lay over everything, and hovered in the air in small particles, like faerie dust. I suddenly found myself feeling incredibly tired, so I lay down on the only piece of furniture in the entire room—a giant, king-sized bed that sat in the corner, across from the window. I lay there gazing at the moonlight, until I suppose I must have dozed off, only to awaken some time later, and realized, with a sickly feeling crawling up my spine, that I was not alone in the room. In the moonlight across from me were three young women, painted heavily with makeup and eye shadow, and dressed like ladies of the evening, in sheer, very short nightgowns – teddies, I guess you'd call them—with very sexy underwear beneath, and very high heels. They were giggling, and speaking – whispering, actually—in Russian. For a moment I thought I was having another weird dream, but then the three of them moved onto the foot of the bed, and I could feel the mattress moving, so I knew it was no dream. They began crawling up the bed toward me in a very seductive manner. They were all very fair-skinned, pale, even. Two had long, blonde hair, and eyes like pale sapphires. The other was a redhead, with dark, piercing eyes. All three had brilliant, white teeth, with long, sharp, needle-like canines, which shone like pearls against the ruby of their voluptuous lips. I found myself longing for them, but at the same time fearful. I felt in my heart a wicked, burning desire that they would kiss me with those red lips. They whispered together, in Russian, and then they all three laughed – such a silvery, musical laugh, but empty somehow, without any real humanity. And then they began to disrobe, until all three were completely naked. I tried to stop them, Mimi, I did! Please believe me! I told them I was engaged, but they just laughed at me. Then, giggling, they stood up together on the bed, and walked to me. I could feel myself cringing away from them, Mimi. I did not give in to them, I swear! I tried to get away, scooting back, as far away as I could get, back to the wall at the very corner of the bed. But they kept coming, giggling and chittering away in Russian. I couldn't understand a word they spoke. And then, finally, when they were standing directly over me, and gazing down upon me with those piercing eyes, they squatted over me, and I felt something wet trickling down on my skin, like warm drops of rain. It tinkled down upon me, and it was very warm. It was then that it struck me: they were urinating! God help me, they were peeing on me! And their pee, it burned, Mimi. It burned! And all I felt was dirty shame and terror.

But at that instant a sudden chill entered the room, and I was conscious of the presence of the Count. And then I saw his tiny, yet strong hands grab the slender necks of the weird sisters, and with a fierce sweep of his arms he hurled the women away from me, sending them crashing into the far wall, where they curled up into a ball and whimpered. And the Count – my God, Mimi, I've never seen such wrath in a person! His mango-colored skin seemed to pulse a deeper shade of orange, his normally blue eyes were blazing red, as if the flames of hellfire burned behind them. His sharp, white teeth champed with rage, and he pointed violently at the women, who were slinking away from him in terror.

"How dare you defile him, you crazy, hormonal

bimbos?" he snarled, his orange jowls flapping like sails in a typhoon. "I have told you, this man belongs to me! You don't touch him until I am finished with my business and have no more use for him! Look at you! Such nasty women! You're disgusting! If you put the three of you together, you'd maybe total a 15. No higher. That's what? A 6 average? Not good. Terrible. You're slobs."

One of the blonde women, cowering in the corner, then hissed at him, speaking in harsh, broken English with a thick Russian accent. "You yourself never loved! You never love!" she wailed.

The Count turned to her and said in that odd tone of his, "Wrong. Fake news. I love my daughter, Ivanka. I kiss her every chance I get. She's tremendously sexy and very, very voluptuous. If she weren't my daughter, I'd…"

The same blonde interrupted him. "Can't you just let us pee on him a little more, and kiss him? We are so thirsty!"

"No!" Trumpula hissed. "I promise you, when I'm done with him, you can pee on him all you want. Kiss him too. But not yet! There is still work to be done!"

"Are we to have nothing tonight?" cried the red-haired one, and she pointed toward a bag which he had thrown upon the floor, and which moved as if there were something alive inside. The Count sighed and nodded his head. The three women jumped forward and, crowding around the bag, opened it, and I heard a low cry come from within it, like the cry of a small, half-smothered child. The women all smiled as they peered into the bag, ruby lips curling back to reveal their needle-sharp teeth, and I heard that high-pitched, tittering laugh come from their red, dripping mouths once again.

"Oh, look!" said one of the blondes. "Sean Spicer!"

Trumpula nodded. "He's a fairly useless human being. You can have him." Then he stood and nodded again at the weird sisters, and the women howled with delight, and huddled around the wriggling sack, and I heard Spicer's high-pitched voice, quaking with fear, call out, "Master? What's happening?" And then, as the women bent over him, I heard the most awful gnashing and tearing sounds, and the little man began screaming, and the women were laughing, laughing and gnashing and slurping and ripping, and then the horror of it all overcame me, and I sank down unconscious.

COUNT TRUMPULA'S TWITTER ACCOUNT

Donald J. Trumpula@RealTrumpula 17th January, 2017, 5:14 a.m.

The spotlight has finally been put on the low-life leakers. They will be caught! That bed really tied the room together. #smellslikerussianasparagus

MIMI MURRAY'S E-MAIL

17th January, 2017; 9:07 a.m.
To: Jonathan
From: Mimi
Subject: Your little pee party

Whoah there, tiger! Skanky Russian pee hookers? A vampire President-Elect crawling around on the walls like Spiderman? That is all just so strange and nasty! Are you on something? Did Trumpula slip some acid in your Wheaties? Or are you just messin' with me? Please let me know, so I can respond appropriately. I think you just need to get out of there and come home. Like, yesterday.

—M

p.s. I found the best Samurai sword on Etsy! It's a Katana – the best kind. I'm going to buy it! Only $800, like new! It's soooo beautiful! ☺ How jealous are you? Like, on a scale of 1-10?

JONATHAN HARKER'S E-MAIL

17th January, 2017; 5:47 p.m.
To: Mimi
From: Jonathan
Subject: Shit just got real!

My dear Mimi, I know you think this is all some sort of sick joke, but I assure you, it's not. It's very, very real, and things just keep getting queerer. After I passed out, I woke up some time later back in my room, lying in bed. I had been undressed and put into my pajamas – by who? The Count? The Russian pee hookers? I can't know for sure. But I was all sweaty and not feeling well at all. It was 4 o'clock in the afternoon. I'd slept all day through the heat, but I did not feel rested. Quite the opposite, in fact. Getting up, I went to my door and, miracle of miracles, it's unlocked! Being as quiet as possible, I opened it and exited out into the stone hallway. The entire palace was dark and silent as the grave. I decided to go to the Count's rooms and see if he's home, so I made my way down that cold, quiet passageway to The Donald's door. I knocked, but there was no answer, so I tried the handle. Locked. Next to his room, there is an open window in the hallway that looks out to the west, at the Intercoastal Waterway. I went to the window and stuck my head out, looking to the right, toward the Count's window. It, too, was open. There is a narrow ledge that runs along the building on that side, protruding between the two windows. Well, I thought, if old Count Trumpula could do it, so could I! I swung my legs out onto the windowsill, one at a time, and climbed out onto the ledge. Turning, I held onto the side of the building and crept my way toward the Count's window. In no time at all, I was there! I climbed in, feet first, and looked around for the Count, but the room was empty. Oddly, there was no bed, just a dresser, a couple of ancient-looking, overstuffed chairs, an old, ornate feinting couch, a couple of side tables and lamps. All of it was covered in a thick layer of dust, except for the three large, flat screens he had mounted on the walls, all three of which were tuned to Fox News. How strange it was, Mimi! And then, even stranger still, I found a great pile of gold in one corner of the room – Russian money, covered with dirt, as though it had recently been dug up out of the ground. None of it, that I could see, was less than three hundred years old! There were also jewels. Rings and bracelets and chains and ornaments, and all of them quite old and stained. In the opposite corner was a closet. I went to the door and opened it, but it wasn't a closet at all. Instead, the door opened to a circular stone stairway, which went steeply down into the bowels of the palace. I descended, moving slowly, because the stairway was very dark, and filled with cobwebs. At the bottom, there was a dark, tunnel-like passage, through which came a sickly stench, like the odor of old earth recently turned over, and death. As I went through the passageway, the smell grew stronger and heavier, and I had to cover my mouth with my hand. Even so, the smell made my eyes water, it was so foul. At last I pulled open a heavy door which stood ajar, and found myself in what looked like the remains of an old, ruined chapel, which had evidently been used as a crypt. The roof was broken, and in three places were steps leading to vaults, but the ground had recently been dug over, and the earth placed in great, wooden boxes. I made a search of the place, even going into the vaults, but there was nothing in the first two except fragments of old coffins and piles of dust. In the third, however, I made a horrifying discovery. It was a long, shiny, rectangular, golden coffin of sorts, with an electrical cord running out of one end, connected to an extension cord, which ran up the wall to the ceiling and then disappeared up into the palace proper. It looked like the coffin of the richest man in the world. I carefully made my way up to the head of the golden coffin, and lifted the lid. And as I raised it, I felt an incredible amount of heat coming from inside. And there, lying naked except for a bright pink Speedo and a pair of matching pink goggles, surrounded by banks of ultraviolet lights, lay the Count! He was either dead or asleep, I couldn't say which, because behind the goggles, his eyes were closed. There was no sign of movement, no pulse, no breath. I bent over him and listened to his hairless orange chest. His skin was very warm to the touch, as he had been tanning, but there was no sound, no beating heart inside the man at all, that I could hear! But then when I stood up and looked down at him, marveling at the amazing burnt umber color of his skin, his eyes suddenly popped open and he rose straight up at me out of the tanning bed/coffin, as if he were being pushed upright by unseen hands. I backed quickly away from him, terrified, stumbling as I scrambled backwards through the dirt to get away. But, my God, Mimi, his face! It looked horrible, so filled with rage and hate, eyes burning red behind the goggles. And then he leaned down and got a bottle of lotion, which he poured into his tiny palm, and began rubbing it all over his skin. Then he held it out to me and said, "Get my back, would you, Harker?" He set the lotion down on the lip of the coffin/tanning bed, and turned around, waiting for me to rub it on him! I got so scared I fled as fast as I could, out of the crypt, and back up the stairs, back into the Count's room. Not wanting to open his door and leave some sign that I'd been there, nosing around his things, I went back out the window, the way I'd come, and crawled back along the ledge to the window in the hallway next to his room. From there I made my way back inside the palace and went up to my room, collapsing into an overstuffed chair, where I sat for a long time, going over everything that I'd just seen, and pondering it all.

COUNT TRUMPULA'S TWITTER ACCOUNT

Donald J. Trumpula@RealTrumpula 17th January, 2017, 5:54 p.m.
Cell service from my coffin is TERRIBLE. The worst! Otherwise I would totally be tweeting something very smart. I have a very good

Donald J. Trumpula@RealTrumpula 17th January, 2017, 5:55 p.m.

brain. You know it, I know it, everybody knows it. Thanks, Verizon! SEE YOU IN COURT! #canyouhearmenow?

MIMI MURRAY'S E-MAIL

17th January, 2017; 11:19 p.m.
To: Jonathan
From: Mimi
Subject: Big news!

Guess what? Lucy and Arthur are engaged! I told you about him, he's the lumberjack from Oregon. Or cowboy? I forget. The whole romance is straight out of a Zane Gray western, whatever he is. Lucy says he's going to take her "out west" for their honeymoon so they can ride the purple sage, or whatever one does out there. Anyway, she invited me out for drinks after work and sprung the news! So exciting! She's asked me to be her maid of honor! Of course I said yes. Lucy's absolutely over the moon. Though she had to break the news to her other suitor – Dr. Seward, the Brit. Poor fellow. I guess he was quite smitten, and took the rejection hard. No date yet, but Lucy says it's to be a short engagement, so you'd better stop dilly-dallying around with Mango Mussolini and come home or they'll be married before we are!

By the way, your last email was very funny, haha. It is a joke, isn't it? I can't even tell anymore. What's REALLY going on down there? I thought this was supposed to be a quick trip? Really, I know you're having quite the time down there with Agent Orange, but don't you think this vampire joke has gone far enough? I miss you!

XXOO

—M

JONATHAN HARKER'S E-MAIL

17th January, 2017; 11:47 p.m.
To: Mimi
From: Jonathan
Subject: I confront the devil

A couple of hours after I got back to my room, after the sun went down, I heard some rattling in the hallway, and, having dressed, I opened my door to investigate. The noise was coming from the dining room downstairs, so I made my way down to find Trumpula, looking alive and well, sitting at his table, with yet another bucket of KFC, cutting into a chicken breast with knife and fork. He paused with the fork halfway to his mouth, a small piece of chicken skewered on the end of it. He frowned up at me, his cornflower blue eyes narrowing to angry slits as his lips kissed at me from the middle of his tangerine face.

"Hello, Harker. Been doing anything... interesting?"

I stared down at him. "I know your secret," I told him softly. "You're a... a vampire!"

His squash-colored cheeks seemed to darken, and he snarled, his gums receding around those sharpened canines. "Wrong. It's a hoax. You people in the media are the WORST. The lowest form of life. Just totally, totally biased!"

"I'm not in the media," I said. "I'm a lawyer."

"Totally biased!" he repeated. "Fake news! Enemy of the American people! That's why your newspaper is FAILING. I'll see you in court! What makes you keep printing such TERRIBLE lies, like 'Global warming is real,' 'Obama was born in America,' and 'Trumpula's a vampire?'"

I pointed at the red baseball cap covering his ridiculous hair. "Well, for starters, you're wearing a hat with a picture of vampire fangs that says 'Make America Suck Again,' and also you're drinking from a mug that says 'World's Greatest Vampire Dad.'"

He glanced down at the mug in his tiny hand. "My gorgeous, sexy daughter, Ivanka, got this for me for Father's Day. She's totally hot. A great, great beauty. She's six feet tall. She's got the best body. She made a lot of money as a model. A tremendous amount. She's very, very voluptuous. If I weren't happily married, and, you know, her FATHER..."

I found myself feeling nauseous, and had to interrupt

him. "Okay, just please, stop talking about how hot you think your daughter is! It's really creeping me out right now."

Trumpula pursed his lips tightly, quietly staring at me, as if it were a terrible strain to not continue. Finally he could contain himself no longer, and blurted out: "I'd totally do her…"

I covered my ears and waved my arms wildly at him. "Eww! Just shut up! Shut up! Shut up! Shut uuuuuuuuuup! What is wrong with you?!? You're seriously making me ill!"

An awkward silence came over us then, as neither of us knew what to say. Finally, after what seemed an interminable time when neither of us spoke, the Count cleared his throat and gestured toward the large chicken bucket. "Want some KFC?" he asked me.

I felt my lip curling in disgust at the thought of sharing his table and breaking bread with such a foul creature. "No," I said, rather bluntly.

"Good!" he spat, pulling the bucket away from me. "Because you can't have any. It's mine!"

I felt a sudden pang of regret, and told him, "Well, now I want some."

He wrapped his arms around the bucket, protecting it, and pursed his lips at me like a petulant child. "Too bad, so sad. Can't have any. All mine." He then reached into the bucket and grabbed a large chicken breast, stuffed it into his mouth and began wolfing it down. Before he had even half-finished that piece, he grabbed another, and shoved it into his mouth as well. Then another.

Another long, awkward silence passed between us as I watched him eat one piece of chicken after another, moaning in near orgasmic delight at how great it tasted. "Mmmm," he cooed. "Delicious! The best. And it's all mine. None for you, loser! Buh-bye now." Finally, as he finished the last piece of chicken, he removed his red cap, and his swooping mane of hair sprang perfectly into place. It seemed to pulse and throb on his orange head. I found myself staring at it, mesmerized by the way it sat there, as if it were a living thing, breathing and watching me, like a small, blond marmot or some other type of rodent. I couldn't take my eyes off of it, and eventually I began to feel dizzy. My eyelids grew heavy and began to droop, lower and lower, until they closed completely and I fell into a deep and dreamless slumber.

COUNT TRUMPULA'S TWITTER ACCOUNT

Donald J. Trumpula@RealTrumpula 18th January, 2017, 2:11 a.m.

@Jonathan Harker: I'm not a vampire. YOUR a vampire! I'm rubber, you're glue, you're words bounce off me and stick to you! #sothere

Trumpula@realTrumpula 18th January, 2017, 2:11 a.m.

J. Harker turned out to be a TOTAL LOSER and TERRIBLE PERSON. Makes me nauseas. You can do better, Hawkins & Co! #sofired

Trumpula@realTrumpula 18th January, 2017, 2:12 a.m.

So-called lawyer J. Harker is a stone cold LOSER with no talent. Lucky my I.Q. is one of the highest and I was able to correct his misteaks.

Trumpula@realTrumpula 18th January, 2017, 2:14 a.m.

Hey TOTAL LOSER J. Harker, I'm not a vampire, but if I were I'd totally be a Robert Pattinson type vampire, cool and sexy, not a creepy

Trumpula@realTrumpula 18th January, 2017, 2:15 a.m.

greesy-haired Gary Oldman type vampire. Yuck! #teamedwardalltheway

Trumpula@realTrumpula 18th January, 2017, 2:16 a.m.

Robert Pattinson, I got a lot of heat for saying you should dump Kristen Stewart—but I was right, like always. She cheated on you like a

Trumpula@realTrumpula 18th January, 2017, 2:16 a.m.

dog and would again. Am I ever wrong? #youcandobetter

Trumpula@realTrumpula 18th January, 2017, 2:17 a.m.

My inauguration as Prez airs live on Fox News Jan. 20. Open invite stands for Robert Pattinson. #MakeAmericaSuckAgain

JONATHAN HARKER'S JOURNAL

18th January, 2017—My phone has disappeared! I suspect the Count has stolen it to keep me from contacting anyone and telling them what I now know: that he is a bloodsucking fiend! A vampire, who rises from the coffin to suck the blood of the living!

I confronted him in the dining room tonight, while he ate a Trump steak with ketchup. (That, in itself, should disqualify him from being President.) When I accused him of taking my phone, he said: "Wrong. It was Obama. He's probably wire-tapping it right now. He's a bad – or sick – guy!" Then he hypnotized me with his hair, and made me sleep. He must have carried me to my room again, for I awoke in my bed in the middle of the night, with no recollection of how I came to be here. Again, it was the sound of the giant bat flapping its wings above that woke me. When I rose, it let out a high-pitched scream, and flew out the window. I got up and went to the window, watched it in the moonlight as it circled, hovering over what appeared to be a row of large, wooden crates laid out in the courtyard below. There were a full dozen of the great boxes – I counted them – and I watched as the bat began defecating into the crates – long, greenish globs of goo hurtling down to land with uncanny precision on its target. Suddenly I remembered what the Count had said about his "process" for producing guano, and his dealings with the Russians. Could it be that the bat is really the Count, having transformed himself somehow? I shudder at the thought! And yet, it *does* look like him, with that strange little poof of swirly blond hair on its head! I watched as the hideous creature filled the wooden crates with its vile droppings. Over and over again it dropped its noxious load into the wooden boxes below, until the crates were all filled to the brim with a foul, steaming cargo. Repulsive, yes, but worth a fortune all the same, for there must be a thousand pounds or more of the putrid stuff. A veritable mother lode of green gold!

Finally, the dark sky began to brighten as the first rays of the morning sun eeked their way through the fading night, and, letting out a mournful screech, the bat circled the courtyard one last time, then fled, descending straight as an arrow for the walls of the palace, disappearing into the window which I had climbed into only yesterday – the Count's window!

Dumbfounded, I stared at the open window which the bat had entered, then, reeling, made my way back to my bed, where I lay for awhile, terrible thoughts running through my head. After a half-hour or so, a loud commotion from the courtyard below drew me back to the window. There, I saw a giant moving van backing up to where the guano crates sat. Loud beeping noises came from the van as it backed its way to the boxes, then stopped. Two men wearing red baseball caps—which looked just like the Count's "Make America Suck Again" hat – exited the truck, opened the back of the van, then set to work sealing the tops of the crates with their heavy, wooden lids, which they nailed into place with hammers. I tried to get their attention, yelling out the window and waving my arms at them, but either they couldn't hear me or were simply ignoring my cries, for they never once even glanced up at me. I ran to the door, intending to run down the stairs and beg them to take me with them, away from this vile place, but my door was once again bolted from the outside. I struggled and heaved at it, to no avail, so I hurried back to the window and cried down to the movers again. But they just went on with their work, completely ignoring me, though I continued hollering and waving my arms, even beating the side of the palace walls below my window with my open hands until they were bruised and raw. It didn't matter. They refused to even look at me. Still, I did not give up, until they loaded the last of the crates, closed the van's door, and drove off. I am overcome with despair!

Same day, later—I am so distraught I couldn't sleep. Just lay on the bed fully dressed, trying to devise a means of escaping this wretched place. After 4 o'clock in the morning, I thought I heard whispering in the hallway, outside my door. I went to it on tiptoe and listened. I heard the voice of the Count:

"Back, back to your own place, you nasty women! Tomorrow night, he's all yours! And then you'll have all the blood, blood coming out of your wherever, believe me." There was a low, high-pitched ripple of women's laughter, and then the hushed voices of the Russian pee hookers as they spoke excitedly in their mother tongue. Then they all joined in a horrible laugh, and I could hear the high heels of the pee hookers clacking on the stone floor as they walked away down that dark corridor.

I went back and threw myself down on my bed. So that is my fate! Tomorrow he is giving me to the pee hookers to be micturated upon until I am dead! Oh, what a horrible fate! To be peed to death by Russian floozies!

I lay there, my mind racing, until I was awakened by the sound of the moving van returning to the courtyard below. Opening my eyes to the splash of bright sunshine that came streaming through my open window, I rose and went to see what was happening. Looking out from my window, I watched as the same two men in the same red "Make America Suck Again" ballcaps got out of the truck and entered the palace. Some minutes later they returned, coming out of the same door carrying the golden coffin/ tanning bed I found the Count in just yesterday. It is him! I am sure of it! They are taking him to Washington, where he assumes the Presidency, and where I have secured him the new estate, where he will prey upon some poor, innocent librarian. Oh, what a fool I've been!

COUNT TRUMPULA'S TWITTER ACCOUNT

Donald J. Trumpula@RealTrumpula 18th January, 2017, 6:54 a.m.

Coffin time is BORING! When I am POTUS in 2 days, all my coffins will have flat screens so I can watch @ Fox&Friends, which is a wonderful show,

Trumpula@realTrumpula 18th January, 2017, 6:55 a.m.

much better than FAKE NEWS CNN! Don Lemon is dumb as a rock! #enemyofAmerica

Trumpula@realTrumpula 18th January, 2017, 8:21 a.m.

Look out Washington, here I come to Make America Suck Again! #draintheswamp

JONATHAN HARKER'S JOURNAL

18th January, 2017 – The Count is gone, I can feel it! The movers have taken him away in his tanning bed/coffin, leaving me to my ghastly fate at the hands of the Russian pee hookers. But there are still a few hours of daylight left for me to save myself. I have decided I will climb out my window and try to scale the palace walls down to the courtyard, and from there make my escape. I don't know if I can make it, but I must try! It is my last hope. These may be the last words I ever write. If so, then goodbye, Mimi, my love! Tell the world my story!

MIMI MURRAY'S E-MAIL

18th January, 2017; 7:22 p.m.
To: Jonathan
From: Mimi
Subject: Big news!

Crap on a mackerel, Jonathan! Where ARE you? I tried calling you like three times today and it just goes straight to voice mail! I know you're busy, sweetie, but call me, ok? I miss you and I'm worried!

xxoo

—M

MIMI MURRAY'S E-MAIL

18th January, 2017; 10:01 p.m.
To: Jonathan
From: Mimi
Subject: Worried!

Just tried calling AGAIN. I'm really starting to freak out, J. Please, please, just call me or text me, ok? I need to hear from you! I need to know what's going on!

—M

THE NOTES OF DONALD J. TRUMPULA AS RECORDED ON OBAMA'S SECRET WIRETAPP SURVEILLANCE SYSTEM

19th January, 2017 – Hello, Barack. It's me again, The Donald, 45th President of the United States. Continuing my totally amazing memoir, "Bite Me: Donald J. Trumpula's Life as the Greatest Vampire President Ever in the History of the Universe. PERIOD!" By Count Donald J. Trumpula.

Chapter Three. The 1830s. We had the Alamo, which was a total disaster, okay? The Alamo was a terrible fort. It was collapsing before the Texans ever got there! The north wall was very porous. I don't know who the contractor was, but I would have withheld payment. I would absolutely not have paid. If Jim Bowie or Davey Crockett had come to me to build their fort, they would be alive today, believe me. I'd have built much better walls for a fraction of the price, and I would have made Santa Ana pay for it. Nobody builds better walls than me, trust me, and I build them very inexpensively. Needless to say, the battle was a complete disaster. Jim Travis was a terrible general. He's no Michael Flynn. That shoddy fort made us look weak.

Then, in the 1840s, William Henry Harrison – a Whig – won the Presidency, and he was very, very mean to Andrew Jackson, a great guy and a swashbuckler with a very bigly heart. And Harrison was a bad guy, very bad guy. Wanted to dismantle everything that Andrew Jackson had done for the country and for the Indians, so at Harrison's inaugural – the Tippecanoe Ball – I bit him in the neck and sucked out half his blood, maybe a little more than that, and 50 days later, he died. A total loser. In 1850, Millard Fillmore, another Whig, came in, and he was okay. He was very big on guano, so we did some deals. The rest of the 1800s, not much happened. It was pretty boring, to tell you the truth. In the 1860s, I played a lot of golf. I would have fought in the Civil War, which I wasn't a fan of, but I had a doctor that gave me a letter – a very strong letter on the heels. They were spurs, heel spurs. They didn't go jingle, jangle, jingle, but it was difficult from the long-term walking standpoint. And I had a very high draft number, phenomenal number. Anyway, I wasn't a fan of the war. So-called "Honest" Abe Lincoln totally divided the country. You know it, I know it, everybody knows it. A terrible leader, Dishonest Abe, and an even worse vampire hunter. He just didn't have IT – a major lightweight with no credibility. Total loser! Sad.

And speaking of the Civil War, I'll tell you, the best land for a golf course is a place I used to play before the Civil War – even during the War – it's called Gettysburg. Great,

great fairways there, and I've tried for years and years to get them to sell that land to me. You know the government has it "protected," which means they grabbed it for themselves, which is ridiculous. So that's one of the things that's high on my list, decommission Gettysburg, get it away from the losers at the National Park Service, and let my people build a fabulous, beautiful resort there so everybody can enjoy it, not just a few history snobs. Trust me, it will be amazing, and many people will be very, very impressed. And, by the way, it's not just Gettysburg. There are many, many pieces of wonderful, tremendous land in this country that the federal government has locked away that should be opened up, like the Grand Canyon, Yosemite, Yellowstone – tremendous land there that we could do some amazing things with.

And now if you'll excuse me, I have to get ready for my inaugural, which is going to be quite yuge, the bigliest inaugural ever, and we're going to get terrific ratings, trust me, but I have to prepare, because I'm the President, and you're not.

PART TWO

WASHINGTON, D.C.

RONALD REAGAN WASHINGTON NATIONAL AIRPORT

Arlington County, Virginia

The Washington Post

January 18, 2017
Page C7

GHOST AIRLINER CRASH-LANDS AT REAGAN NATIONAL AIRPORT

Boeing 727 Was Empty Except For Pilot,
Who Was Found Dead At the Controls

(Arlington County, Virginia) – A Boeing 727 jet airliner made a miraculous crash-landing at Reagan National Airport Tuesday evening, at 8:21 p.m.

According to officials, no one was aboard the plane, save for the as yet unidentified pilot, who was found dead in the cockpit, with his hands tied to the controls. Preliminary reports indicate the pilot died of severe trauma, and not natural causes such as a heart attack.

One witness, who asked not to be identified, said that the pilot died from blood loss attributed to a "gaping" wound to his throat, which appeared to have been "ripped open by ravenous wolves."

Several eye witnesses reported seeing a large orange ape-like creature, possible an Orangutan, leap from the plane and run off into a wooded area south of the airport. A search was underway for the Orangutan, but so far no trace of the creature has been found.

FAA officials said that the Boeing 727 originated in Palm Beach, Fla. An FAA spokesperson said investigators were still trying to ascertain who owns the plane.

Adding to the mystery was a report, circulated early Wednesday morning, that the Arlington County Coroner's Office estimated that the pilot had died at least an hour *before* the airliner crash-landed at Reagan National.

"I've never anything like it in my 21 years in law enforcement," said a shaken Deputy Chuck Massara of the Arlington County Sheriff's Department. He added that police do not suspect terrorism.

"Right now we've got a lot more questions than answers," Massara said.

Strange Cargo

Authorities immediately cordoned off the runway where the jet came to rest, and all flights to and from the airport had been cancelled as of Wednesday morning.

"The airport is shut down until further notice," said FAA spokesman Whitney Snow.

Department of Homeland Security officials were seen swarming around the plane late Tuesday evening, and several large wooden containers were removed from the plane's cargo hold and taken to an undisclosed location for testing.

A DHS Spokesperson said that the containers contained an unidentified foreign substance, and that federal authorities were conducting preliminary tests on-site to determine whether the materials found inside the containers posed a threat to public safety.

At a press conference Wednesday morning, Snow told reporters that the plane had been "cleared," and that the chemicals found inside the containers was "guano." When asked for a clarification, Snow confirmed that the plane was carrying "a very large amount of fresh bat excrement," worth several hundred thousand dollars.

Guano is highly sought after by organic farmers as fertilizer, and sells for up to $15 per pound on the open market.

The Washington Post

January 19, 2017
Page C5

CRASHED GHOST JET OWNED BY RUSSIAN GUANO TYCOON

(Arlington County, Virginia) – FAA officials announced that the Boeing 727 – the so-called "ghost plane"—that crash-landed Tuesday evening at Reagan National Airport is owned by Russian oligarch Dmitri Gerkov, a guano tycoon known as the "Baron of Bat (dung)." Gerkov, reached at his home in Moscow, refused to comment.

FAA officials also said that the flight originated in Palm

Beach, Fla., earlier Tuesday evening. The Department of Homeland Security released a statement saying that the plane was carrying more than 40,000 pounds of guano in "several hundred" wooden crates, a payload estimated to be worth more than $500,000 on the open market. Guano is highly sought after by organic farmers as fertilizer.

Meanwhile, Arlington County Animal Control Officer Fred "Crash" Ferch said that a search for a large Orangutan allegedly seen jumping from the plane and running in the direction of a large wooded area south of the airport had not been successful. "We've found no orangutans or monkeys of any kind," he said. "Just a lot of rats, some possums, couple of snakes, a porcupine, and one Congressman who apparently had quite a weekend."

Several eye witnesses reported seeing a large orange ape, possibly an Orangutan, leaping from the plane immediately after it crash-landed Tuesday, and running off into a wooded area south of the airport.

According to officials, no one was aboard the plane, save for the as yet unidentified pilot, who was found dead in the cockpit, with his hands tied to the controls. Arlington County Sheriff Ted Kohler refused to comment on reports that the pilot's throat appeared to have been "ripped open by ravenous wolves," saying only that the investigation was "ongoing."

DR. JOHN SEWARD'S MEDICAL DIARY

19th January, 2017 – Had a very interesting patient admitted to the asylum today. His name is Seanfield. I went to his room to introduce myself. The poor fellow was sitting in the corner in a highly agitated state, gibbering to himself in his high-pitched, squeaky voice. His face was nearly purple, and I couldn't understand anything he said.

"Hello, Seanfield," I said, standing at the door while the attendant locked it behind me. "I am Doctor Seward. I'm a clinical psychologist and the Director of the asylum. I'm here to help you."

"I don't want to talk to you," he mumbled. "You don't count. The Master is at hand!"

He then disgusted me when a giant blowfly buzzed into the room through the barred windows, and Seanfield suddenly leapt up like a panther and caught it, held it for a moment between his forefinger and thumb, and before I knew what he was going to do, stuffed it into his mouth and ate it! When I asked him why he did it, he explained that it had been sent to him by "the Master" – whoever that is – and it was very good and wholesome, that it was life, strong life, and by eating that life it gave life to him. Then he stood and walked to the window. Looking out across the green grounds below, he began yelling, "The Master is at hand! The Master is coming, he is coming, and he is beautiful!" And then he began tearing off his clothes, stripping right down to his tighty-whitey underpants, all the while screaming, "Master! I live to serve you! Let me serve you, Master! I am here to do your bidding! Let me serve you! I await your command, Master!"

I went to him and gently placed my hand on his pale shoulder. "Come, Seanfield," I said in as soothing a voice as I could muster. "Come and sit."

Eventually I got him to calm down and come with me to

the small cot in the corner of his room, where we sat together in silence. I was waiting for him to speak. Instead he began softly sobbing. And then, before I could even react, he suddenly fell to the floor on his hands and knees and began crawling after a large cockroach that was scurrying towards the corner. He managed to catch it, then held it up and looked at it, smiling as it dangled there in front of him, and then he opened his mouth and ate it, chewed a couple of times and then swallowed it down. "Thank you, Master! Thank you!" he cried.

I got up and went to him, lifting him to his feet, and he seemed much calmer. He turned to me, smiling, a slow trickle of drool oozing out the corner of his open mouth, and he said, in a soft, peaceful voice, "The Master is coming. He is coming. He is coming to make America suck again!"

MIMI MURRAY'S WORK E-MAIL

19th January, 2017; 6:37 p.m.
To: Lucy
From: Mimi
Subject: Jonathan

Joy! Joy! Joy! But not all joy. I've got news of Jonathan! I've just got off the phone with his boss – Mr. Hawkins—John's been hospitalized in West Palm Beach! Apparently he had an accident at Mar-a-Lago – they say he fell three stories from a window! He's suffering from broken bones, contusions, and a "violent brain fever" – whatever that is – but doctors say he's going to be all right! He's been unconscious for two days, and only today woke up and identified himself.

Apparently he arrived at the hospital with no ID, and no one knew who he was, which explains why I couldn't reach him, and why no one was contacted for so long. Anyway, I just talked to the boss, and she's giving me indefinite leave. I'm flying down there today, so I'll have to miss not only Kung Fu practice, but your dinner party tonight. I'm so sorry, Lucy, I was so looking forward to it. I'm sure it will be wonderful, you are such a fantastic hostess! ☺

I will call you from Florida and fill you in on all details. Somehow I am sure Count Kumquat had something to do with this!

Talk soon! Give my best to Arthur! Hugs!

—M

P.S. Please explain my absence to Mr. Hirai. Also, would you mind taking care of Kat? Thank you!

COUNT TRUMPULA'S TWITTER ACCOUNT

Trumpula@realTrumpula 19th January, 2017, 8:04 p.m.

Terrible! Just found out that it was Obama on the grassy knoll! A NEW LOW!!!

JONATHAN HARKER'S JOURNAL

19th January, 2017 – My dear Mimi, it was so good to hear your voice on the telephone just now, and such a relief to know that you are on your way here. I miss you so terribly, and can't wait to see you!

I need to put the events of my last day at Mar-a-Lago down on paper, while I am still able to recall them in detail.

On that last, fateful evening at Trumpula's palm-lined palace, after the Count had gone, I spent the day trying to work up enough courage to attempt to climb out the window and down the side of the palace. I couldn't bring myself to do it, until I heard the Russian pee hookers outside my door, scratching and giggling, and I knew my time was up. So I went out the window! I was able to get enough of a handhold on the stone to climb and sort of slide my way down to the next floor below, but as I continued on, inching my way, my foot slipped and I lost my grip, and plummeted three stories to the ground below! Luckily, I landed in some shrubberies, which cushioned my fall a bit, but the doctors here tell me I broke three ribs – one of which punctured my lung—my collarbone, and sprained both ankles, as well as many cuts and abrasions. Somehow I did not pass out, and managed, after a time and much struggle filled with excruciating pain, to get to my feet. I limped through the courtyard and around the palace to the public entrance – where the club is located – and managed to make it inside. My God, Mimi, you should have seen it! Like a European palace! Gold leaf everywhere, with 15th-century tiles paving the entrance, painted frescoes on marble walls, and a baby grand piano in the corner. It was majestic, and filled with the so-called "beautiful people," the filthy rich, the men all fat and suntanned, dressed in golf or tennis clothes, the women adorned with jewels, but all of them wearing that same, stupid red ballcap that the Count wore, with the same logo: Make America Suck Again, and a picture of sharp fangs. And all of them, Mimi, walking around as if in a trance, mumbling "Master! Where is the Master? Why has the Master forsaken us?" And lording above them all, an oil painting of a smiling Trumpula wearing a natty white tennis sweater, watching us from his perch above the fireplace. And there I was, bleeding from a head wound, in horrible pain, limping like a madman, and all these wealthy idiots could do was talk about how they pined for their "master!" One fellow – a boob in an expensive suit and one of those ridiculous red "Make America Suck Again" caps—obviously drunk and carrying a croquet mallet, just kept telling me how Trumpula is a "man of the people" and how he'll "drain the swamp." He was sobbing and blubbering like a baby for his "Lord and Master." I grabbed his cellphone and dialed 9-1-1 before collapsing on a red, velvet Louis XIV feinting couch. I woke up here in the hospital two days later, suffering from what the doctors called "brain fever," as well as all the other injuries I mentioned. They tell me I am lucky to be alive. They don't know the half of it, Mimi! I am counting the minutes until you arrive!

LUCY WESTENRA'S E-MAIL

19th January, 2017; 7:04 p.m.
To: Mimi
From: Lucy
Subject: Jonathan

Oh, Mimi, yes, joy, joy, joy! I am so happy to hear that Jonathan's alright! Though his injuries sound terrible! What an awful ordeal! But it sounds as though he'll be okay, right? Please don't worry about anything here. Of course I will miss you terribly, but don't worry about Kat, I will take care of your little furball. Feel free to call if you need anything at all, or just want to talk! And do let me know how Jonathan is doing! Much love and hugs!

—Lucy

MIMI MURRAY'S E-MAIL

19th January, 2017; 11:04 p.m.
To: Lucy
From: Mimi
Subject: Jonathan

Dear Lucy,

Thank you so much for your kind wishes, and for taking care of Kat. You don't know how relieved it makes me feel. I arrived in Palm Beach around 9 o'clock and came straight to the hospital. Poor Jonathan! He's so thin and pale and weak-looking! Bandages everywhere – including one wrapped around his head. He's sleeping now. This ordeal has taken a lot out of him, but the doctors assure me he will make a full recovery, though it will be a long road, with all his broken bones, and the "brain fever," whatever that is.

J's boss, Mr. Hawkins, was just here. He flew all the way down here just to check up on J personally. Such a dear, sweet old fellow! I told him I blame the Angry Mango for everything. He said the firm hasn't heard from Trumpula and he doesn't know what to make of it. Jonathan tells us the Count was not at Mar-a-Lago at the time of the accident, but other than that he hasn't said much to me about any of it. I get the feeling he's hiding the truth to protect me. Sigh. Anyway, J just woke up, so I'd better sign off for now. Just wanted to check in, and say thank you again for helping me out in this time. You are such a wonderful friend!

Talk soon! Love and hugs to you and your cowboy!

—M

LUCY WESTENRA'S E-MAIL

20th January, 2017; 1:41 a.m.
To: Mimi
From: Lucy
Subject: Jonathan

Dearest Mimi, I am happy to be able to help. How are you holding up? And how is Jonathan doing? Better, I'm sure, now that you are there! ☺

I stopped by your apartment and fed Kat and sat with him a few minutes, petting him. He purred like an engine and sat on my lap. He's such a sweetie! I wished I could have stayed longer, or brought him home with me, but I had the dinner party. Tonight I will go and get him and keep him with me until you return, if that is okay with you.

The party went very well. Although Dr. Seward was there and he told the most disgusting stories about a patient of his. Apparently this man was just recently admitted to the asylum where Dr. Seward works, and he spends all of his time catching bugs and eating them! Imagine, telling stories like that at dinner! You'd think a doctor would have more sense! I probably shouldn't have invited him, but he has been very kind to me, and, surprisingly, he and Arthur (my fireman, not a cowboy, you silly girl!) actually hit it off quite well, strangely enough. Arthur was most fascinated by his horrible stories about this patient – Seanfield, I think the Dr. called him. I guess they were pretty interesting at that. He says this Seanfield fellow goes on and on about some "Master" who he serves. The poor wretch believes it is this Master who sends him the cockroaches and flies and spiders to eat – lives, he says, for him to consume, which, by consuming them makes Seanfield stronger. In his poor, deluded mind, anyway. He sounds quite mad, in a harmless sort of way.

Well, I suppose I should end this screed and try to get some sleep. I'm feeling a bit run down today. Probably just the stress of everything that's been going on – the engagement, and the dinner party and all. Plus it's been very busy at the library. We all miss you! ☺

It's very stormy here tonight, the wind keeps battering my window, and a strange fog seems to have enveloped the place. And I keep hearing a fluttering and scratching at my window, like a bird is out there, trying to get in! So weird.

Love and hugs to both of you!

—Lucy

MIMI MURRAY'S E-MAIL

20th January, 2017; 4:22 p.m.
To: Lucy
From: Mimi
Subject: Jonathan

Dear Lucy,

I'm so glad the dinner party went well. I'm sorry I couldn't be there! Your friend, Dr. Seward, sounds interesting?

Jonathan seems to be a bit better today. He was able to eat a little bit for breakfast before going back to sleep. He sleeps a lot, which is to be expected after his ordeal, the doctors say. He hasn't talked yet about what happened, and I've not pressed him, as he is still too weak and the doctors fear a relapse of the "brain fever." At one point J woke up and asked for his journal, which was in a drawer by his bedside, along with his clothes. The nurse told me it's all he had with him when he was admitted. He asked me to read the last three entries, so I did. I'm not sure what to believe, Lucy. It's horrific. Seriously. Like something out of a bad horror movie. I'm not sure how much of it to even believe – if what he wrote was a result of the "brain fever" or what. But it jibes with what he was telling me about what was going on down here with that two-bit wall salesman. I need to think about what to do next. But at least there's plenty of time for *that* here.

Well, the doctor is here so I should go. Thanks again for everything, Lucy. Give Kat a big hug for me. And one for yourself. And get some rest! I know how stressful things are right now, but you need to take care of yourself, girl!

Talk soon,
—M

P.S. I just remembered, today is the inauguration! I'm sure traffic will be horrendous! Maybe wait til after it's cleared to get Kat? Sorry! And THANK YOU!

DR. SEWARD'S MEDICAL DIARY

20th January, 2017 – Very disturbing episode today with my new patient, Seanfield. I went to his room to check on him, and found him stripped down once again to his underpants, pacing up and down in a most agitated state, drooling and gibbering. As soon as I entered, I asked him what was the matter. He flashed at me in a most aggressive manner, snarling, "The Master is coming to secure our borders!"

When I asked him who this "master" was, he jumped at me, grabbing me by the throat in a death grip. He seemed to have extraordinary strength in his little hands and arms, and for a moment I feared he might squeeze the life out of me! He was drooling – the spittle from his mouth flying everywhere—and wild as a great ape. He accused me of "opposing" his Master. "You are all dumb idiots! Arrogant elitists!" he spat at me. "You cannot stop him, you jackass! The Master is at hand! He is coming to build his wall, and secure our borders, and all those who oppose him shall be cast aside, and suffer a most horrible fate!"

Just as I was about to pass out from his throttling, the orderly burst in and laid hands on Seanfield, but the lunatic swatted him aside as if he were one of his precious little flies. The orderly went tumbling into the wall and crumpled to the ground in a daze. Then three or four more orderlies came rushing in and grabbed the maniac, finally succeeding in pulling him off of me. After a long struggle with much grunting and shouting and biting and flailing of limbs, and spittle flying and curses hurled about, they managed to subdue the poor, deranged crackbrain and put him in a straitjacket.

Once I'd got my wind back, I asked them to leave so I could speak alone with the patient. He had, by this time, becalmed himself greatly, and was lying quietly on his cot, all wrapped up in the straitjacket like a bug in a cocoon. I sat down on a chair on the opposite side of the room and looked at him, and he at me. He spoke calmly, as if he were a completely different person from the lunatic who'd just tried to choke the life out of me.

"The Master is at hand," he said, in a low voice, nearly a whisper. "The Master is coming! He is coming to make America suck again!"

Suddenly he went quiet, as his eyes were drawn to a fat, black spider which just then dropped down in front of him on its silken web from the ceiling, dangling just inches from his mouth. Seanfield looked at the bug, his beady, black eyes going cross-eyed as he stared at the wriggling insect. And then the lunatic opened his mouth and out sprang his tongue, quick as a lizard's, snatched the spider from his web and sucked it into his mouth, lickety splat! He swallowed, and a look of pure bliss came over his lunatic face. Licking his lips, he gazed at the window. "Thank you, Master!" he cried. "Thank you! I am your slave, Master!" Then he made a disgusting noise from his nether regions, befouled the air with a sickening odor, and soiled himself.

COUNT TRUMPULA'S TWITTER ACCOUNT

Trumpula@RealTrumpula 20th January, 2017, 4:14 a.m.

My arm is feeling tired from waving at millions of fans at my yuge inaugural. Biggest inaugural in history! Make America Suck Again!

LUCY WESTENRA'S E-MAIL

21st January, 2017; 11:13 a.m.
To: Mimi
From: Lucy
Subject: The Inaugural

Mimi! So glad Jonathan's improving. I do hope you guys will be coming home soon! I miss you so much! I can't begin to understand what he's been through. Btw, traffic was no problem yesterday when I went for Kat. I thought it would be beastly, but there was hardly any. The inauguration was puny compared to Obama's. Hardly anybody showed up! Tee-hee!

Kat's with me now and fine. Love him!

Talk soon,
Lucy

COUNT TRUMPULA'S TWITTER ACCOUNT

Trumpula@RealTrumpula 21st January, 2017, 11:31 a.m.

The liberal media's claim of small crowds at my inaugural is FAKE NEWS! Bigliest crowd ever! Yuge. Don't believe the lying photos!

The Washington Post

January 26, 2017
Page C11

TIC TAC GROPER CLAIMS ANOTHER VICTIM NEAR WHITE HOUSE

For the third time in a week, a young woman has been attacked within blocks of the White House, forcibly kissed and sexually assaulted by an assailant police have dubbed "The Tic Tac Groper."

A man wearing a long, black cape over a dark suit approached the 26-year-old woman, who was waiting for a bus by 67th Road and Yellowstone Boulevard, after 10 p.m. on Wednesday, stuck his hand beneath the woman's skirt and forcibly kissed her while fondling her, police say. As in two other similar incidents over the past week, the woman said that, just before grabbing her, the man shook a package of Tic Tacs into his hand and popped some of the popular breath mints into his mouth.

The suspect is described as being 6-foot-2, between 50

and 60 years old, with an orange complexion and a mane of strange, swooping blond hair.

In the two previous incidents, the women were also bitten in the neck. A police spokesman said it has not been determined whether the three attacks were related to the discovery of the body of a 24-year-old woman near the White House last Friday. In that case, the woman had fresh bite marks on her neck, and had been almost completely drained of blood.

THE NOTES OF DONALD J. TRUMPULA AS RECORDED ON OBAMA'S SECRET WIRETAPP SURVEILLANCE SYSTEM

27th January, 2017 – Hello, Barack. It's me again, The Donald, 45th President of the United States. I'm here in the White House, which is a real dump. Total rat trap. Disgusting.

Anyway, getting back to my memoir. Chapter Four. The 1900s. 1912, to be exact, I was on the Titanic when the lookout said there was an iceberg, but I knew it was Fake News. It wasn't an iceberg, there was never an iceberg. It was terrorists. ISIS, disguised as an iceberg. It was an isisberg. And since Obama and Hillary created ISIS, then it was their fault the isisberg sunk the Titanic. But I managed to survive, because I'm a survivor. I got in one of the lifeboats, I was very, very fortunate to be able to throw those old ladies and children out into the ocean and make enough room for me and my trunks and suitcases. It's called winning, okay? So I survived, went back to New York, and I made a killing on Wall Street. This was during the Crash in '29. I got some very good advice and acted on it, sold short, and things went really, really well for me. Amazingly good. And it was a tremendous thing for the country, a yuge success, everyone was thrilled during that time, nobody was depressed. Everybody was so happy, until 1932, and the Lindbergh baby. Boy, you kidnap one tiny baby to feed to your vampire brides and the whole country goes crazy! Just insane. The Fake News media wouldn't shut up about this baby. "Oh, you can't feed the Lindbergh baby to a bunch of vampire hookers! It's not politically correct! Boohoo!" So I had to lay low for awhile after that.

Then, just when the economy was going along so well and everything was so great, this loser, FDR becomes President. This guy, total failure and a cripple, was a complete socialist. You've got to see this guy, rolling around, he's rolling around in this chair, [unintelligible noises] *"Aaaaah, I can't walk, I had polio! Help me stand up! Aaaahhh!"* [more unintelligible noises]. And this loser got us into World War II, which I wasn't a fan of. Sure, you had some Nazis on one side, and some of them were bad people, but you had a group on the other side that came charging in without a permit, and they were very, very violent. It was an egregious display of hatred and violence on many sides. On many sides. But I totally would have gone if it hadn't been for my heels. I would have gone, and I would have been great. I'd have been one of the first to storm the beaches at Normandy, maybe parachuted in behind enemy lines, captured many key, strategic areas. I would have won many, many medals, terrific medals, the best. Yuge medals. I've always wanted to get the Purple Heart. But I had a doctor that gave me a letter – a very,

very strong letter on the heels. And I had a very high draft number, phenomenal number. So I spent most of the war years, like most Americans, golfing, and just laying low until the whole Lindbergh baby thing blew over, which I knew it would. Just as I predicted with my very good brain. I happen to be a person who knows how life works, and I'm almost always right. I said I was going to win the election, in fact I was number one the entire route, in the primaries, from the day I announced. I was number one. But I said I was going to win and I won easily. Remember, they said there was no way to get to 270? Well, I ended up at 306. I had election night, 306. The biggest landslide in the history of the election. Yuge landslide. Brexit, I predicted Brexit, the day before the event. I said no, Brexit is going to happen, and everybody laughed, you laughed, and then Brexit happened. Many, many things. They turn out to be right. And I must be doing something right, because I'm President and you're not. But you're still here, somewhere, with your illegal wire tapp, spying on me from my nose hair clipper or my electric foot massager. What a bad, sick guy you are, Barack. Kellyanne says you put the microphone in the electric can opener, but I checked at lunch and I couldn't find it. But I will. I don't know why you're tapping my wires, Barack. Probably because you're angry that I've vowed to repeal Obamacare and replace it with something really, really terrific. I've got the most amazing health care plan, believe me. Here's what we're going to do: I'm going to bite everyone and make them vampires, and then no one will get sick because they'll already be dead. Or undead, technically. What could be better than that? They'll always be in perfect health, just like me, because they'll be vampires, and they won't need healthcare, so problem solved. And here's the best part, are you ready for this, Barack? The best part is, since they're not technically dead, they're still eligible to vote. And who do you guess they'd vote for, my minions? Trumpula. And now if you'll excuse me, I have other Presidential things to do, like meet with my terrific National Security Adviser Michael Flynn, who's the best National Security Adviser ever with absolutely no Russian ties, period. Everyone keeps talking about my Russian ties. It's so ridiculous. Don't they know all my products come from China? Ties, shirts, cufflinks, capes. Find the leakers, that's the real story. Oh, and if you plan to follow me, tonight, I'll be going to the store to pick up some more Tic Tacs for later, when I'll be moving on this new girl I've been moving on very, very heavily lately. Her name's Lucy, and she's a solid 8, 8 ½.

Well, that's all I have time for right now, Barack. I'm having dinner tonight with FBI Director Comey, who's a terrible showboat and a grandstander. In fact, he's such a showboat that, after dinner, I'm going to make him sing "Ol' Man River" from the tremendous Broadway musical, *Show Boat*. We'll see how he does. If he does a good job, I might not fire him. I'll let you know. Wait, you'll be taping the whole thing, so you'll hear it all. Never mind. You're a bad, or sick guy, Barack.

COUNT TRUMPULA'S TWITTER ACCOUNT

Donald J. Trumpula@realTrumpula 28th January, 2017, 1:13 a.m.

Had dinner with FBI Director Comey. After dessert I asked him to pinky swear his undying loyalty to me, and promise that I'm not under

Donald J. Trumpula@realTrumpula 28th January, 2017, 1:14 a.m.

investigation for being a vampire. He declined. Then I made him sing Ol' Man River, and, guess what? He totally nailed it! #Showboat

LUCY WESTENRA'S E-MAIL

28th January, 2017; 11:13 a.m.
To: Mimi
From: Lucy
Subject: Weird Dream

Dear Mimi, how are you both? Will you be able to come home soon? My fingers are crossed. I miss you terribly! The library – heck, Washington!—just isn't the same without you.

I must tell you about the awful dream I had last night! It was so real and strange, I feel as if it really happened! I was asleep in my bed, and again I heard the strange flapping at my window. And then Kat – who I have brought home with me, and was sleeping with me in the bed – let out a frightened cry, leapt from the bed and darted out of the room. I got up and went to the window and looked out, and there was a big bat, with a strange swooping tuft of blondish hair on its head, buffeting its wings against the window! Something – some strange force that seemed to be controlling my motions – compelled me to open the window, and when I did the bat flew past me in a ghostly flutter, and then suddenly I felt a strange chill come over my back and shoulders, and somehow I was aware that I wasn't alone. I turned around and there was a man, dressed in a dark suit, with a long, flowing cape draped around his shoulders. His face had an orange glow, and his hair looked like a dead fox or some other small creature – a woodchuck, perhaps—had crawled up to rest on top of his head and died there. It was blond in color, and combed forward in a strange fashion. Kind of poofy. It was horrid, and yet I found myself strangely drawn to it, unable to stop staring at it. I felt a powerful urge to touch it and run my fingers through it. I moved toward him, reaching out to feel this hideous hair. He took some Tic Tacs out of his pocket and shook a couple into his mouth. And then suddenly his eyes – which were like a pair of tiny blueberries above puffy eye sacs when I first saw them – turned red as fiery coals, and he sprang forward like a wolf, reached down with his tiny, clawlike hand, and grabbed me by my lady bits! In my dream, I felt so ashamed! I remember thinking that I love Arthur, and what would he think? But yet I felt powerless to stop this horrid man, as if I were hypnotized or something. He began kissing me with his awful lips, pushing me back against the wall and forcing his tongue down my throat. He was much bigger than me, a looming figure, quite strong. In this strange dream, I snapped out of my trance finally, and managed to unpin myself, pushed him away and said, "No!" very forcefully, and then I slapped him across his orange face. He got very angry and hissed at me like some foul beast. "Oh, come on!" he spat. Then he flashed a leering smile and said in a very odd but confident tone, "You know we're going to have an affair, don't you? Trust me, I'm, like, a smart person." I told him I would never have an affair with him, and that he disgusted me. He said, "It's because of what they said about me in the liberal, elite media, isn't it? Fake news! Or was it Obama? Did Obama badmouth me to you? He tapped my phones, you know. Like Nixon/Watergate!" And then he began moving his head in a way that accentuated his ghastly hair, and again I became mesmerized looking at it. The next thing I knew, he was on me again, thrusting his hips and grinding against me as he kissed me on the mouth. And then his mouth moved to my neck, and that is all I remember.

I woke this morning feeling horribly weak. My face is ghostly pale, and my throat hurts. I wonder if I'm anemic? On top of everything else, I must have got a chest cold. I can't seem to get enough air in my lungs. I wish Arthur were here, but he had to go back to Oregon, as his mother is ill.

Oh, but I have good news! We have a wedding date! May 25! So mark your calendar, missy! I have so much to do. I must rest and get well. I hope I don't have those horrible nightmares again.

Give my love to Jonathan, and call if you want to chat. Love and hugs, hugs and love!

—Lucy

COUNT TRUMPULA'S TWITTER ACCOUNT

Donald J. Trumpula@realTrumpula 28th January, 2017, 7:24 p.m.

Terrible! First Obama tapps my phones, now I find out that he's cock-blocking me with the chicks! A NEW LOW!!!

Donald J. Trumpula@realTrumpula 28th January, 2017, 7:25 p.m.

It's O.K. I got to her anyway. I moved on her like a bitch, grabbed her by the pussy. She loved it. She's under my spell now.

MIMI MURRAY'S E-MAIL

29th January, 2017; 6:01 p.m.
To: Lucy
From: Mimi
Subject: Jonathan

Dear Lucy,

So strange about your dream! It's like an exact replica of the dreams J described having at Hair Fuhrer's palace – including the bat! How weird is that?!? And, don't you recognize the creepy dude in your dream? Your description of him: the orange face, the swirly blond hair, the pure, undiluted narcissism? The unbridled rich white guy entitlement? It's

Trumpula! Totally! The part about him grabbin' your lady parts? That's the Cheeto's *move*, girl! I guess it makes sense that he's invaded your subconscious (ew!), he's all anyone talks about anymore. But again: *ew!* Who wants that pervy baby-fingered man-toddler all up in their head?

Soooooo excited about your wedding date! May 25 – perfect! Where will it be, do you know yet? You must let me help with the planning, dah-ling! I'll do all your grunt work. Delegate, Lucy, delegate!

I am blowing you air kisses from Florida.

Get better!

—M

P.S. How's Kat? Give him a kiss for me! I miss the little furball!

LUCY WESTENRA'S EMAIL

30th January, 2017; 10:48 a.m.
To: Mimi
From: Lucy
Subject: Another strange occurrence

OMG! You're right! It IS Trumpula in my dream! Eeek! So gross! Is it really true that Jonathan had similar dreams? That is so strange! How is he? Close to being well enough to come home? I hope so!

Last night I had the dream again. Awoke to the sound of scratching and flapping at my window, and again I dreamt that I rose from my bed and went to the window, and opened it. And again, the bat with the funny hair flitted into my room and disappeared, and, just like last time, the man with the swirly hair appeared as if from nowhere. Again he popped a couple of Tic Tacs into his mouth, then, just like before, he lunged at me and grabbed my lady garden! I tried to fight him off, as he thrust his hips at me and jammed his tongue down my throat. I scratched him and beat him with my arms. I told him I could never be his, that he didn't respect women. Then he spoke to me in that same odd and supremely confident way, with the ultimate air of entitlement. He said: "I happen to be, in my own way, a feminist. I've won many awards. Yuge awards. Bigly." And then he pointed his strange head of hair at me, and once again I felt myself falling under its weird, hairy spell. I felt his lips trailing down my neck, and then something sharp. And then the blackness.

I woke again in an awful state. I look hideous, M! My face has lost all its color, and the pain in my throat is worse. It hurts to breathe, and I can't seem to get any oxygen. I've called in sick again. Oh, I miss Arthur, and you, too, Mimi! I know that you have your own crisis right now, with Jonathan's accident and all, but I do wish you would hurry and come home. I'm all alone here, and I can't help but feel as if my life were draining away from me. I'm so tired. I must try and sleep.

Kat is fine! Such a love! He curls up with me at night and purrs and purrs. I may not be able to give him up when you return! ☺

Goodbye for now, dah-ling. I miss you!

Lucy

P.S. Oh, in answer to your question, we do NOT have a venue for the wedding yet. Any suggestions? Arthur keeps bringing up the Watergate, cause, ya know. But *yuck!* Just no. I'd really love to get the Decatur House and have a garden wedding. Swoon.

COUNT TRUMPULA'S TWITTER ACCOUNT

Donald J. Trumpula@RealTrumpula 1st February, 2017, 6:15 a.m.

In spirit of fairness, I hearby declare February Orange History Month. To celebrate, I built hotels on St. James Place, NY & Tenn Aves.

MIMI MURRAY'S E-MAIL

2nd February, 2017; 3:36 p.m.
To: Lucy
From: Mimi
Re: Another strange occurrence

Hello Lucy! Jonathan seems to be improving a bit each day. Thanks for asking. The doctors say he's still a ways away from being discharged and being able to travel, so it's going to be awhile yet, I'm afraid.

You dreamed of the Gropenfuhrer AGAIN? My, you've got it bad, girl! ☺ (Gag me with a rusty stomach pump!). Though I shouldn't talk. When I was in grade school, I used to dream about Jimmy Carter. Something about those manly-yet-sensitive peanut-farmin' hands! (Don't you dare breathe a word!). I don't know why. It had been years since he was President at that point.

But seriously, Luce, have you seen a doctor about the shortness of breath or any of the other symptoms (lack of energy)? You should. Please do! Don't make me come back there and kick your ginger ass! Speaking of which, I don't suppose you've been to Kung Fu lately, or been working out at all? I try to do some of the exercises when I can, when the nurses aren't around, or before bed in my hotel room. I brought my sword down with me, and I haven't accidentally stabbed anyone yet! It's actually a lot of fun training with it. I wish J would hurry up and heal so we could leave and get back to our lives.

Re. wedding venues, by all means, the Decatur House! That would be loverly. Put your dainty little foot down, girlfriend! We only get married once (hopefully). Nix to the Watergate! (get it? Nix-on? ☺) Though I'll admit it does have a certain G. Gordon Liddyish charm… But, yeah, just no.

See you soon, I hope!

—M

COUNT TRUMPULA'S TWITTER ACCOUNT

Tweet from Trumpula@realTrumpula
5th February, 2017, 7:41 a.m.

Terrible! Just found out that Obama faked the moon landing! A NEW LOW!!!

DR. SEWARD'S DIARY

11th February, 2017 – The case of the imbecile Seanfield grows more interesting by the day. I think I shall have to invent a new classification of lunatic for him. He has certain qualities which are very highly developed: paranoia, selfishness, deviousnesss, childishness, and purpose. I wish I knew what was the object of the latter. He doesn't eat, doesn't read, doesn't socialize with any of the other inmates. Instead he spends his days and all his energy catching flies and imprisoning them in a collection of mason jars he keeps lined along the wall on the floor of his padded room. He started with one jar, but kept asking for more as his fly collection grew. Now they number more than 30, and the number of his little buzzing pets must be in the hundreds. When I came in today I found him berating his "pets," kneeling down in his underpants, holding one of the jars to his purplish face. He was laughing at them and calling them "dumb idiots" and "liberal elites." I must watch him.

13th February, 2017 – My patient has a new hallucination. Now he believes that he is a radio broadcaster! He has saved a pickle from his daily meals and pretends that it is a microphone. I found him sitting in his chair in only his underpants, holding the pickle to his mouth and speaking into it in a loud, clear, though comically high-pitched voice.

"And now you have the alt-radical left with their master plan to damage and destroy the Master. The Washington D.C. swamp is rising up. It is colluding and viciously fighting to take down the 45th president and his entire administration. It's that serious. And they're starting with Michael Flynn. Claiming that he met with the Russians. It's pure poppycock! Ever since the Master showed himself, there's been this liberal witch hunt. They are salivating! Nobody connected to him is off limits. They want everybody! They're a bunch of dumb idiots!"

COUNT TRUMPULA'S TWITTER ACCOUNT

Donald J. Trumpula@RealTrumpula 11th February, 2017, 5:53 a.m.

The Democrats had to come up with a story as to why they lost the election so badly (306), so they made up a story – Vampires! Fake news!

Donald J. Trumpula@RealTrumpula 11th February, 2017, 6:07 a.m.

Orange History Month Fact: Oompa Loompa's favorite food is cocoa beans. Oompity doompity, losers!

MIMI MURRAY'S E-MAIL (unopened)

13th February, 2017; 11:08 p.m.
To: Lucy
From: Mimi
Re: Where'd you go?

Hey Lucy! Whazzup, girl? You went dark! Haven't heard from you in a coon's age. Is everything okay? Are you feeling better? Still dreaming about the Xenophobic Sweet Potato? (sorry) (not really!) ☺

Did Arthur come and sweep you away? Have you eloped, you bad girl? You better not have!

I'm still stuck here in J's hospital room. He's improving, slowly. Still no ETA on his discharge. Oh, that sounded nasty. ;)

Give me a jingle, mmmk?

Love to Kat!

—M

P.S. How's work? Do I even still have a job there, or have they all forgotten me?

COUNT TRUMPULA'S TWITTER ACCOUNT

Tweet from Trumpula@realTrumpula
14th February, 2017, 10:52 p.m.

Asked Comey today if he could see his way clear to rubbing some bronzer on my back, where it's hard to reach. He refused. What a nut job!

DR. SEWARD'S MEDICAL DIARY

16th February, 2017 – Patient Seanfield has turned his attention now to spiders, and has got several big fellows in a box. He feeds them the flies that he collected, the number of which has been decimated now. As he sends the flies to their doom, he laughs and laughs, and taunts them, saying, "See what happens, you jackasses, when you oppose the Master? See what happens? Arrogant elitists! Dumb idiots! Dumb, dumb idiots!"

18th February, 2017 – Seanfield continues to feed his spiders. One, in particular, he seems to pay special attention to. He has named this spider "Obama," after our former President. I found him this morning holding his spider Obama up by one of his legs and berating it most forcefully. "I'll tell you what, you jackass. I have an offer for you, Barrack Hussein Obama. Here it is. Now that my Master is in the White House, I will charter a private plane to take you and your family on a one-way trip to the country of your choice. You pick. You want to go to Canada? I'll pay for you to go to Canada. You want to go home to Kenya? I'll pay for you to go to Kenya. Jakarta, where you went to school back in the day? You can go back there. Anywhere you want to go. I'll put the finest food: caviar, champagne, you name it. I have just one stipulation: you can't come back. Well, what do you say? Nothing? You have no response? What a dumb idiot!"

COUNT TRUMPULA'S TWITTER ACCOUNT

Tweet from Trumpula@realTrumpula 19ᵗʰ February, 2017, 6:03 a.m.

Terrible! Just found out that it was Obama who let the dogs out! Bad (or possibly sick) guy! A NEW LOW!!!

DR. SEWARD'S DIARY

20ᵗʰ February, 2017 – Found Seanfield broadcasting into his pickle again today. He was shouting about the "Fake news" and "liberal elites." He had taken all of his clothes off except his underpants, and dressed the pillow from his bed in his pants and shirt. Then he propped his pillow up as if it were a person, and "interviewed" it, calling it "Obama." I felt sorry for the poor thing, however, as he didn't let it get a word in edgewise. He just kept yelling at "him," accusing him of being a "secret Muslim" and calling him a "dumb idiot" over and over.

COUNT TRUMPULA'S TWITTER ACCOUNT

Tweet from Trumpula@realTrumpula 20ᵗʰ February, 2017, 6:24 a.m.

Orange History Month Fact: Orange Sherbet is easily the best Sherbet, and it's not even close. Rainbow-colored isn't a real flavor, give me

Donald J. Trumpula@RealTrumpula 20th February, 2017, 6:25 a.m.

a break. Raspberry is a no-talent loser!!

DR. SEWARD'S DIARY

22nd February, 2017 – Patient Seanfield's spiders are now nearly as plentiful as his flies were a few short weeks ago, and today I told him that he must get rid of them. He looked very sad at this, and begged me to let him keep them. I gave in, and told him that he could keep a few, but that the rest had to go. He seemed happy to hear that he could at least keep some. Then he disgusted me by opening one of the boxes where he keeps his spiders, grabbing a handful, and popping them into his mouth. He grinned stupidly at me as he chewed them up and swallowed. I asked him why he did this, and he said because they were lives, and the Master wanted him to grow stronger by consuming them. "The Master has promised to make me immortal!" he said, breathlessly.

He keeps a little notebook, which he is always scribbling in. Pages and pages of it are filled with figures, generally single digits added in batches, and then the totals added in batches again, as if he is keeping some account. I have no idea what these numbers signify, whether they have something to do with his little "pets," or are merely the outpourings of his diseased mind. I will endeavor to learn more about these figures.

COUNT TRUMPULA'S TWITTER ACCOUNT

Donald J. Trumpula@RealTrumpula 23rd February, 2017, 6:47 a.m.

Orange History Month Fact: If you take out the millions who voted illegally, I easily won Orange County, CA in a yuge landslide. MASA!

DR. SEWARD'S MEDICAL DIARY

25th February, 2017 – Seanfield has managed to get a sparrow, and has already partially trained it, apparently by feeding his spiders to it. Not all of them, for he's kept his favorites, like the spider he calls "Obama," safe from his newest pet. Those he has kept are well-fed and fat, as he continues to use his own food to bring in the flies, which he then feeds to the spiders.

COUNT TRUMPULA'S TWITTER ACCOUNT

Donald J. Trumpula@RealTrumpula 25th February, 2017, 1:28 a.m.

Looking at presidential portraits in the White House. Some First Ladies too. Hannah Van Buren – solid 9. I'd totally grab her by the pussy.

Donald J. Trumpula@realTrumpula 25th February, 2017, 1:33 a.m.

Eleanor Roosevelt – what a dog! Not even a 1! Betty Ford: 5. Martha Washington: 2 ½. I cannot tell a lie: you could do better, George.

Donald J. Trumpula@realTrumpula 25th February, 2017, 1:35 a.m.

I like Ike. Total winner. Yuge for America. But Mamie, not so much. I rate her a solid 3.

Donald J. Trumpula@realTrumpula 25th February, 2017, 1:37 a.m.

Jackie Kennedy was a great beauty. The face is a solid 8. The legs are maybe a bit less. From the midsection to the shoulders, though,

Donald J. Trumpula@realTrumpula 25th February, 2017, 1:38 a.m.

only a 4. The boobs are terrible. They look like 2 light bulbs coming out of a body. Overall, I would give Jackie a solid 7.

Donald J. Trumpula@realTrumpula 25th February, 2017, 1:40 a.m.

Hillary Clinton. Married to maybe the worst sexist ever. I give her a 4. But on a full moon, Hairy Hillary turns into a total dog. A 1!

Donald J. Trumpula@realTrumpula 25th February, 2017, 1:43 a.m.

She's a Werewolf, people! If she couldn't satisfy her husband, what made her think she could satisfy America? Sad. #nastywoman

Donald J. Trumpula@realTrumpula 25th February, 2017, 1:47 a.m.

Mary Todd Lincoln: a real looser with the face of a dog! You take a look at her, she's a slob. And she was crazy to boot! A solid 1.

Donald J. Trumpula@realTrumpula 25th February, 2017, 1:49 a.m.

Abe Lincoln, let's be honest. A very ugly man. One of the most overrated presidents and a TERRIBLE vampire hunter! Weak!

Donald J. Trumpula @realTrumpula 25th February, 2017, 1:50 a.m.

Abe Lincoln, totally overrated. He's not a hero. He's a hero because he got assassinated. I like people who weren't assassinated, OK?

MIMI MURRAY'S JOURNAL

25th February, 2017 – Dear Diary, I know we haven't spoken in years, so, umm, this is all a bit awkward. But we're both adults now, so I'm hoping we can keep this professional. I've been cooped up here in Jonathan's hospital room for weeks with hardly anyone to talk to, with Jonathan asleep so much of the time. His ordeal with Cantaloupe Caligula has really taken a lot out of him mentally. But the doctors assure me he is getting better, so yay for that!

I'm also awfully worried about Lucy, as she's gone off the grid for the past couple of weeks, not returning my texts or emails, not answering her phone. But the other day I called and Arthur answered. He was just back from Oregon, where he's been tending to his sick mother. He said Lucy's quite ill herself, and they'd just got back from her doctor's, where she'd undergone a battery of tests. Of course, they won't know anything till the results come back, but apparently the doctors are flummoxed. They thought she might be anemic, and Arthur mentioned Lyme disease, which is quite worrisome. Arthur is a dear, very concerned about Lucy. He said she apologized for not answering my emails or calls, but that she's been too weak to write or talk on the phone, not sleeping well, and still plagued by her terrible nightmares featuring Marmalade Mao. Of course I told him no apologies necessary. He did tell me that Kat is fine, which is good. I was worried about my little furball, too! So much to worry about lately! Anyway, he promised to call if anything serious develops. That's all for now, dear diary. Let's hope for better news next time.

COUNT TRUMPULA'S TWITTER ACCOUNT

Donald J. Trumpula@RealTrumpula 28th February, 2017, 6:03 a.m.

Orange History Month Fact: Finding Nemo would have been a much better film without no-talent Ellen DeGeneres, a Hillary flunky who lost big!

DR. SEWARD'S MEDICAL DIARY

7th March, 2017 – Patient Seanfield progresses in his master plan, whatever that is. He has a whole colony of sparrows now, and his flies and spiders are almost completely obliterated. When I came in he ran to me and, falling to the floor, groveled before me, fawning and pleading. When I asked what he wanted, he said, with a sort of rapture in his voice, "A kitten! A nice, soft, cuddly playful little kitten, that I can play with, and teach, and feed – and feed – and feed!"

12th March, 2017 – Visited Seanfield very early this morning, and found him up and humming a tune, seeming quite happy. He was spreading out his sugar, which he had saved, on the windowsill, evidently beginning his fly-catching again. I looked around for his birds, but not seeing them, asked him where they were. He replied, without looking at me, that they had all flown away. I noticed a few feathers about the room, and what looked like a drop of blood on his pillow. I said nothing, but went and told the orderly on duty to keep a close eye on him, and report to me if he did anything odd. Well, odder.

12th March, 2017 – About two hours after I'd left Seanfield, I received a phone call from the infirmary informing that the patient had been quite ill and had vomited up a flock of feathers.

COUNT TRUMPULA'S TWITTER ACCOUNT

Donald J. Trumpula@RealTrumpula 12th March, 2017, 6:15 a.m.

Very nice full moon tonight. Where is Hairy Hillary? Why is Comey not investigating? She's a WEREWOLF!!!

MIMI MURRAY'S JOURNAL

12th March, 2017 – Dear Diary, Jonathan improving daily. Doctors say he's on schedule to be discharged soon. Fingers crossed! Guess that's the best I can hope for. Meanwhile, though, Lucy seems to be in the doldrums. I received a phone call from Arthur today, who's very worried, the poor boy. He said all tests came back negative – including for

Lyme Disease – which is a relief, but now her doctor thinks she should see a psychiatrist. I suggested he give Dr. Seward a call, as Lucy seems to think quite highly of him. Arthur seemed unsure of what to do, but he said he'd consider it.

DR. SEWARD'S DIARY

15th March, 2017 – I received an urgent phone call from Arthur Holmwood today. He's just recently returned from out west, where he was tending to his sick mother, and found dear Lucy quite ill herself. He asked me to come over at once and examine her. I informed him that I am a psychiatrist, not a physician, but he insisted, saying that Lucy had already been to see her doctor, who had performed a number of tests and found nothing they could pinpoint. He said he believes the poor girl's illness may be more mental than physical. Of course I could not refuse, so I cancelled my appointments for the rest of the day and drove straight to Lucy's apartment.

Holmwood let me in. He's a large, rugged fellow from some cowboy town out west – Oregon, I believe. He clapped me roughly on the back and said he was happy to see me, then led me in to Lucy's bed chamber.

I found her lying in her bed, looking quite peaked, but I did not see the usual signs of anemia. She complains of difficulty in breathing, of being tired all the time, and heavy, lethargic sleep, with dreams that frighten her. When asked about these dreams, she said they are all much the same: a giant bat with an unusual tuft of blondish hair on its head comes flapping and scratching at her window. She rises from her bed and opens the window, and the bat flies in, but then disappears. She then feels a chill, and a presence behind her, whereupon she turns to see a man in a dark cape – always the same man – with an orange complexion and a strange mane of "swirly" blond hair, like the bat's only much larger, of course. Lucy says that, in her dreams, she is always mesmerized by this man's swirling head of hair, drawn to it as if it holds some strange powers of its own, so that she becomes helpless in its presence. The man then pops some Tic Tacs into his mouth and attacks her in a very vile and vulgar manner, grabbing her by the nether regions and forcing himself upon her. He speaks quite crudely to her during the attack – things of a sexual nature which she finds most embarrassing. Curiously, she says that, in her dreams, the man often also speaks of things political, railing against the "liberal media" and "fake news," and accusing former President Obama of spying on him and tapping his phones. Well, if this doesn't put the "ink" in coink-i-dink! My patient, Seanfield, makes many of these same outlandish complaints, even using the same phrases in some instances, such as "liberal elite media" and "fake news!"

I drew a very small amount of blood from the poor girl – I dare not draw more as she already appears to have lost a great deal, though no one seems to have the foggiest notion how—and will send it to the lab for analysis. I wrote a prescription for a mild sleeping pill. Before leaving, I noticed her rubbing at a black velvet band which she wore around her neck. When I asked to see beneath it, she readily obliged, pulling the band out so I could peek at her throat. Just over the external jugular vein there are two punctures, not large, but not wholesome-looking either. There is no sign of infection, but the edges are white and worn-looking, and a bit puffy. When I asked about it, she said she had no knowledge of how she came to suffer the wound. If I did not know better, I would say this was a bite wound of some wild animal. I did not say any of this to poor Lucy, instead just gave her a reassuring nod, gave her some cream to ensure against infection and a band-aid to put over the wound. I then told her to get plenty of rest, and left her in her room.

On my way out, Holmwood – who seems very concerned – queried me pointedly. "Well," said he, "what do you think, Doc?"

"I'm not sure," I responded. "She is extremely peaked, as if she has lost a great deal of blood. Those marks on her throat. Do you have any idea how they got there?"

He shook his head and said no, only that he had seen a tiny drop of blood on the collar of her night dress.

I nodded, for I had noticed this as well. I told him I would send Lucy's blood to the lab immediately for a full work-up. "I'll contact you as soon as the results come in," I told him, and left.

DR. SEWARD'S DIARY

17th March, 2017 – Lucy's bloodwork has come back clean; there are no signs of anything abnormal, including anemia. This leaves me scratching my head. Surely there must be some explanation as to why the poor girl has lost so much blood. It was then that I decided to contact my old friend and mentor, Professor Bernard Van Helsing, who knows as much about obscure diseases as anyone in the world. It's true, he is a bit of an eccentric, but I believe if anyone can get to the bottom of this strange matter, it is Bernie.

THE NOTES OF DONALD J. TRUMPULA AS RECORDED ON OBAMA'S SECRET WIRETAPP SURVEILLANCE SYSTEM

17th March, 2017 – Hello, Barack. It's me again, The Donald, 45th President of the United States. I'm here to record Chapter Five of my memoir on your secret wiretap machine. The continuation of "Bite Me: Donald J. Trumpula's Life as the Greatest Vampire President Ever in the History of the Universe. PERIOD!" by Count Donald J. Trumpula.

I want to go back to the 1940s for a minute. The Japanese bombed Pearl Harbor, which made my good friend Andrew Jackson very, very angry. He was a swashbuckler, Andrew Jackson, and he had a bigly heart. Yuge. And you had Hitler, who was bad, okay, but at least he didn't sink to using chemical weapons on his own people, even when he took the Jews to the Holocaust Center, where they did some bad things, I'm sure, and perhaps played some ping-pong, maybe some pickup basketball, had their barmitzvahs, that kind of thing. Whatever people do in a center. But at least Hitler was a leader, unlike what we had in this country when you were in charge, Barack. And you know he was very popular in Germany. He had very high approval ratings. You have to give him credit. He was like 44 or 45 when he took over, you know, it's pretty amazing when you think of it. How does he do that? He goes in, he takes over, and all of a sudden he's the boss. It's incredible. He wiped out the unions, the communists. He wiped out this one, that one. I mean, the guy didn't play games. And he dealt with some tough people. A lot of people, I'm sure, tried to take that power away, whether it was von Stuffenberg, von Puffenstuff, whoever. And he was able to do it, so obviously, he's a pretty smart cookie. Yeah, sure, he was tough on the Jews. Very very tough. But I think there's blame on both sides, okay? Both sides. The Jews were very, very violent. What about the Jews who came charging at the German soldiers in the Warsaw ghetto with guns and clubs? Came charging in without a permit. Do they have any semblance of guilt? I think they do. I met with Hitler. I was honored to meet with him, Hitler, I went over there in 1945, met with him shortly before he died. And I told him, "Look, Adolf, you're doing a great job, amazing job. But you don't have to deal with a Constitution like ours, which is a very tough system, very archaic system. It's a really bad thing for the country." And he agreed with me. Like I said, smart cookie. And I have to say, Eva Braun, total fox. I gave her an 8, 8 ½. I moved on her, and maybe I failed, maybe not. I'm not going to say anything further. Just that I did try and fuck her. She was newly married to Adolf. And I moved on her very heavily. I took her out pill shopping. She wanted to get some cyanide pills. I said, "I'll show you where they have some nice cyanide pills." And I moved on her like a bitch. I blitzkrieged her, you might say. I said, "I better use some gum," because still, no Tic Tacs. And I just start kissing. It's like a magnet. Just kiss. I don't even wait. When you're a star, they let you do anything. I grabbed her by the muschi — which is what the Germans call it. Anyway, I gave her a little love bite on the neck area, annexed her blood, and she died.

And Hitler was so devastated, he shot himself. Sad. And you know, I still keep a copy of his speeches by my bed to this day. Amazing, isn't it? I've had a lot of amazing experiences. Many people are very impressed.

DR. SEWARD'S DIARY

18th March, 2017 – I met my old friend, Professor Van Helsing, at the asylum early in the morning. It has been some time since I have seen Bernie, but he is much the same. A bit balder, perhaps, with what hair he has left as unkempt as ever, grown quite white now, and retreating back over his great, shiny forehead. And yet he is as full of youthful vigor as ever, with the energy of a much younger man. He came bounding into my office like a dynamo, speaking in a very loud and forceful voice.

"Jack, you old son of a gun!" he smiled broadly, clapping me on the back. "Good to see you, my boy! Now, let's get this show on the road! What you tell me about this friend of yours, this poor girl, it's simply unacceptable! We must correct it! And remember, my good friend, real change never occurs from the top down, but always from the bottom up!"

We drove immediately over to Lucy's apartment, where I introduced Bernie to Holmwood, as Lucy was still in bed. Arthur seemed very happy to see such an eminent expert. "Professor Van Helsing, it is an honor to meet you sir. Thank you so much for taking the time to examine Lucy at such short notice." He extended his giant hand for Bernie to shake, and seemed quite surprised at Van Helsing's grip.

"Not at all, not at all!" Van Helsing barked, smiling

warmly. "Health care must be recognized as a right for all citizens, not a privilege for the top 1 percent! And one thing, young man: call me Bernie! Now, show me to the patient! Let's get this show on the road!"

Holmwood led us into Lucy's room, where we found her lying in her bed, looking much the same: pale as a ghost, and breathing erratically, eyes closed, but with a pained expression on her beautiful white face.

Van Helsing then set about examining Lucy quite carefully. When I showed him the small marks on her neck, I heard a deep hiss of indrawn breath as Bernie gazed on the tiny punctures. Throughout the examination, Lucy lay motionless, eyes closed, and did not seem to have the strength to speak. Then Van Helsing beckoned to Holmwood and I, and we went quietly out of the room. The instant we had closed the door, Bernie swung his arms out above his shoulders, like an owl flapping its wings.

"Let me be very, very clear," he said, his eyes wide behind the lenses of his glasses. "This girl's life is in grave danger. What has happened to her is morally reprehensible. For her, the American dream has become a nightmare. What I am about to tell you may shock and astound you. But you should not be shocked and astounded. You should be mad as hell, my friends, and ready to start a revolution! This girl has been attacked... by a wampyre!"

Arthur looked at him skeptically. "A wampeer?"

"A Vampire!" said Bernie. "Nosferatu. A creature that is both dead and undead. What has happened is totally unacceptable. This vampire is waging a war against women, and let me be very clear, it is not a war that we are going to allow him to win!"

I do not mind telling you, dear reader, that my first thought was that my old friend, Professor Van Helsing, is a crazy-pants cuckoo bird! As if he could read my thoughts, Bernie raised his fist and shook it violently at me. "My friend, the ones that are crazy enough to think they can change the world are the ones that do! I tell you, this girl is the victim of a vampire! A reprehensible creature of the night, who rises from the grave and sucks the blood of the living in order to prolong its own unholy existence, much like the top one percent in this country have been sucking the lifeblood of the poor and the middle class since the mid 1980s! We must act quickly and decisively to rid the world of this scourge, if we are to save poor Lucy's life."

Holmwood looked at me as if to question my sanity at bringing such a fruitcake into his and Lucy's lives. His reaction was not lost on the Professor. "What? You don't believe me? You think I'm nuts? I'll show you nuts, my friends! Look here…" He led us back into Lucy's room, to the side of her bed, and pointed at the poor, sleeping girl. "That young woman's lost a lot of blood. Where did it go? No blood on her bed, no blood on her clothes, no blood on the floor, no blood on the walls. No blood anywhere! Where's the blood? Where did it go? I'll tell you where it went: right into the mouth of that filthy bloodsucking vampire, that's where! You saw the marks on her throat. If that wasn't the mark of the wampyre, then I'll be a monkey's uncle!"

Holmwood stared at the Professor, dumbfounded, as Bernie headed for the door. "Come, Jack," he said to me. "There isn't a moment to lose! I must consult my books on the occult, and find out how best to deal with this reprehensible creature." He opened the door, then paused, turning to Arthur. "My dear Mr. Holmwood, you must stay with Lucy all night tonight and watch over her. Do not let her out of your sight for even a minute. And, whatever you do, don't open the window!" And then out he went, heading for the car, with me following behind, trying to catch up.

Van Helsing was strangely silent as I drove us back to the asylum. He was obviously brooding, thinking about poor Lucy, and feeling quite glum it seemed, so I invited him up to my office for a drink.

"This is very serious business, my friend," he said, shaking his head woefully as I poured us each a glass of Pimm's No. 1. "If a vampire is too undead to die, it is too undead to exist."

I shrugged, rolling my eyes slightly as I handed him a glass.

He looked at the orange liqueur in the tumbler. "What the hell is this?" he said.

"Pimm's Cup, No. 1," I said, taking a sip. He did the same and smiled. "You're sure about this theory?" I asked him. "You really believe it is a nosferatu that has sucked the blood out of our dear Lucy?"

Before he could answer, my phone rang. It was one of the nurses attending the patient Seanfield. She was quite upset, and asked that I come down at once to his room. I hung up.

"I'm sorry," I said to Bernie. "One of my patients. A most interesting case. The man is quite mad. Zoophagous. He believes he has an invisible Master who supplies him with lives in the form of insects and other small creatures to consume. Apparently he caught a rat, and did something disgusting to it."

Van Helsing's eyes narrowed as he stared at me. "No kidding?" he said, putting his glass down.

"Yes. Bit the damn thing in the neck and drank its…" I felt the color drain from my face as it struck me.

"Don't tell me!" said Bernie. "He drank its blood! Am I right?"

I felt a bit sick to my stomach, and sat down heavily in my office chair. "Yes," I said. "He drank its blood."

"Well, what are we waiting for?" Bernie bellowed, heading for the door. "Let's go meet this meshugah rat-biting bastard!"

"Yes," I said, weakly. "I'm coming."

We made our way down to Seanfield's room, where we found the poor wretch pantless and barefoot, bound in a straitjacket, sitting back on his cot, his smiling, contented face smeared red with blood and bits of rat fur. As soon as we entered the room, however, the smile disappeared, and he stood up, staring intently at Professor Van Helsing. "It's you!" he said, waddling awkwardly in his straitjacket over to Bernie. "You're the pinko liberal who Crooked Hillary stole the dummycrat nomination from! And then you endorsed her, you coward! Are you here to be interviewed on my radio show? Well, you're too late, you dumb idiot! I already did my show today!" Then he tossed his head back and laughed so hard he fell over backwards and began rolling about on the floor in hysterics. "What a jackass!" he laughed. "You came all the way to my studio for nothing! Hahaha!"

"The man's obviously bonkers," Bernie whispered to me. "Ask him about this Master of his."

I pulled up a chair and sat, facing Seanfield, who remained on the floor in convulsions. "Seanfield," I said. "Have you heard from your Master today?"

Suddenly the lunatic stopped thrashing about and went dead silent. He wriggled his body into a sitting position and looked up at me, his beady, dark little eyes growing wide. "Oh, yes!" he said. "The Master sent me a nice, juicy rat for supper!"

"And for what purpose did he send you this rat?" I asked.

"For its life," hissed Seanfield. "It's life!"

The Professor took a step toward the poor, demented fellow. "And how do you go about… accepting this life?"

"What a dumb question," spat Seanfield. "Everybody knows that, you dumb idiot. The blood. The blood is the life!"

"And, where is your Master now?" asked Bernie.

Seanfield's face seemed to go blank, his mouth opened and he cast his eyes toward the window. "He is close at hand," he said softly. "The Master is close! He is coming! He is coming to…" His eyes widened as he went suddenly silent. Then he crawled over to his cot feet-first, like a crab, and, rolling onto his back, slid his feet under the bed and used his toes to grasp a red cap he had hidden there. Displaying great physical dexterity, he rocked back, raising his legs above his head, and managed to put the hat on top of his head. Then he beamed at us proudly, smiling the thoughtless smile of the imbecile. "You see?" he said, rolling his eyes up toward the cap. "He is going to make America suck again!"

"My God!" said Van Helsing. "Look at the hat, Jack! Look at the logo!"

Due to the dim light, I had to lean over closer to Seanfield to make out the insignia on his cap, but when I saw what it was, it made me gasp. On the hat was a picture of a pair of sharp fangs, and in white letters, the phrase, "Make America Suck Again."

"Seanfield," I said. "Where did you get that hat?"

The poor wretch turned his head and gazed back at the window. "The Master brought it to me."

Van Helsing cast me a sharp glance, sparks dancing in his eyes. "He visited you, the Master?" he asked Seanfield.

Seanfield snorted loudly. "Of course, you jackass. How else would he bring me a hat?"

I ignored his crude insult. "You have not had any visitors, Seanfield. I checked."

The lunatic snorted again, his eyes still fixed on the window. "The Master visits me when no one is looking. He comes through the window. He brings me lives!"

Bernie moved closer to Seanfield, squatting down until he was just inches from the madman. "Mr. Seanfield, can you describe your Master for me? What does he look like? Is he young or old? Is he tall, short, fat, skinny? Does he walk with a limp? What color are his eyes? What color is his hair? Is he Caucasian? African-American? Jew? Gentile?"

Suddenly Seanfield turned to Van Helsing, his eyes bulging out of his purple face. "The blood is the life!" he howled, lunging at the Professor's neck. "The blood is the life!"

Bernie fell backward onto his back with Seanfield on top of him trying to bite his neck. Luckily, bound as he was by the straitjacket, the maniac could not use his hands in the attack, and Van Helsing was able to keep him at bay until the orderly and I grabbed Seanfield by the straps of the jacket, and lifted him off the Professor before he could do any damage.

"Holy guacamole!" gasped Bernie as I helped him up. "The man's a total loony tunes!"

As the orderlies tied Seanfield to his bed with leather straps, I took Bernie by the arm and led him out of there and up to my office, where I sat him down on a sofa and gave him another glass of Pimm's to calm his nerves.

"Tell me, Jack," said Bernie after downing the Pimm's in one gulp. "When was Seanfield first committed to the asylum?"

"Let me see," I said, checking my records. "Yes, here it is. Almost three weeks ago, on January 18th."

The Professor rubbed his chin. "Hmmm. That's quite a coincidence. Yes, sir. Quite a coincidence!"

"What's a coincidence?" I asked.

Van Helsing looked at me with a deadly serious expression. "It is a remarkable concurrence of events or circumstances without apparent causal connection. Like when a Wall Street executive gives a large donation to his elected representative in congress, and then that same Wall Street executive bilks John Q. Public out of his life savings and destroys the economy. Does that Wall Street executive get arrested? Does he go to jail? No. Is that a coincidence? I don't think so."

"No!" I said. "I mean, what is coincidental about the date of poor Seanfield's arrival to this asylum?"

But Van Helsing was already crossing my office in long, loping strides, heading for the door. "I'll tell you tomorrow!"

he hollered over his shoulder. "Get some sleep, my friend. You're going to need it!"

MIMI MURRAY'S JOURNAL

18th March, 2017 – Dear Diary, Jonathan's finally being discharged Monday morning, in just two days! I've booked us a flight home for that afternoon. We will be going straight to the airport and leaving Florida behind, hopefully forever. Not that it hasn't been fun, Sunshine State, but, well, it hasn't been fun. I called Lucy to tell her the good news. Arthur answered, and said she was still too weak to come to the phone. He said he took my advice after our last conversation and called Dr. Seward, who was just as flummoxed as Lucy's doctor, so he called in a friend of his, a Professor Van Helsing, who sounds quite eminent, though a bit eccentric, perhaps. Arthur seems to think he may be a bit of a crackpot, though he's much too polite to say it straight out. I told him I'd be over to see Lucy and pick up Kat probably Tuesday, as I'm sure Jonathan will be all worn out after the flight. So, definitely a good news/bad news kind of day, Diary. Just between you and me, I'm starting to get very worried about Lucy. I'm conjuring up all my good vibes and sending them her way, if good vibes even exist in Florida.

COUNT TRUMPULA'S TWITTER ACCOUNT

Donald J. Trumpula@RealTrumpula 19th March, 2017, 6:08 a.m.

Why is it that the Fake News rarely reports on Hillary's whereabouts when there's a full moon? She's a werewolf, and she has FLEAS!

DR. SEWARD'S DIARY

19th March, 2017 – Van Helsing called me early in the morning and said he would meet me at Lucy's apartment. By the time I arrived, Bernie was already there, sitting with Holmwood at Lucy's kitchen table, drinking coffee and peering at a laptop that sat on the table between them. His hair looked as if he'd driven through a carwash in a convertible with the top down.

They assured me that Lucy was much improved, having slept relatively peacefully, for the most part, without disturbance, thanks to Arthur. She did, however, seem to suffer from a strange nightmare in the wee hours of the morning. Arthur described how she'd suddenly sat bolt upright in her sleep, with her arms outstretched and beckoning toward the window. Arthur spoke to her, but she seemed not to notice, and, even though her eyes were wide open, he said she didn't seem to see him at all, just stared at the window, moaning softly, until she collapsed back onto her pillows, asleep.

At the Professor's urging, Arthur told me about another strange occurrence during the night, when he heard an odd flapping noise, like that of a bird's wings, beating repeatedly just outside Lucy's bedroom window.

"But," said Arthur, "when I went to the window and

looked out, I saw it wasn't any bird, it was a bat! A big, ugly bat with a weird tuft of blond hair on its head."

"Good God!" I said. "Just as Lucy described from her dreams! You actually saw it?"

"Damn straight," said Arthur.

"But that's not the half of it!" said Van Helsing. "Show him the e-mails, Arthur."

I walked around behind them to see the screen, as the Professor explained. "Lucy sent some emails to her friend, Mimi, before she was stricken ill, in which she describes dreaming about being visited by the strange, blond-haired bat, and then being attacked by a vulgar, orange-skinned man with blond, swirly hair."

"Yes, yes," I said, scrolling through her emails to Mimi. "She told me about these dreams as well." I felt the color drain from my face as I got to the part in her email where she described being attacked by the man with the mesmerizing hair. "Sweet fancy Moses!" I exclaimed. "She describes this, this pumpkin-colored creature… biting her neck like a…."

"Yes!" shouted Bernie, waving his finger in the air. "Say it! Like a vampire! Only it wasn't a dream! It was real! It was a wampyre, the undead, sucking the lifeblood from her neck!"

Speechless, I looked from the Professor to Holmwood, who looked forlorn, the poor fellow. It was bad enough when his fiancée was just under the weather, but now here was the Professor suggesting that Lucy was the victim of some supernatural bloodsucking demon of the night. He shook his head. "Yeah, but these emails don't prove anything, other than Lucy saw the same strange bat that I did last night. That image must have been in her subconscious to create the man with the poofy hair in her dreams. What I care about now is how to get rid of this damned bat? What if that thing flew in and bit her while she slept? Could be it's given her some sorta disease. What can we do to protect her?"

Van Helsing's eyes grew small and hard behind his glass lenses. He leapt to his feet and began to pace up and down the room, lost in thought. Finally, after wearing a trail in the carpet, he stopped and looked at us. "Tell me, Arthur. When was it that Lucy first became ill?"

Holmwood rubbed his chin, as if he were trying to extract the information from his stubble. "I guess it was a couple of weeks ago. Right after..."

"Right after the inaugural!" yelled Bernie, waving his finger around again. "I'm right, aren't I?"

Arthur stared at the Professor, his face a mask of puzzlement. "I guess."

Bernie jabbed his finger as if he were trying to pop an invisible balloon. "Aha! Just as I thought! The pieces of the jigsaw puzzle are coming together! Gentlemen, if I am correct about the identity of this vampire, then I believe there is a way to protect your Lucy. Arthur, where is the nearest market?"

Arthur responded that there was one at the corner, just down the street. Bernie said he would be right back, and bounded out of the apartment in a mad rush. A few minutes later he returned with two large shopping bags bulging with newspapers and periodicals. His hair stuck up in all directions.

"Quick!" he said, handing us each an armload of papers. "Put these around your dear Lucy! Surround her bed with the news!"

Holmwood and I just stared at him, flabbergasted, as he burst into Lucy's bedroom, moved to the window and began taping pages of *The Washington Post* all over Lucy's windows.

"Professor," I said. "Are you sure you are feeling all right? Perhaps you'd like to lie down and rest a bit."

Bernie looked at me over his shoulder, smiling widely. "Ahh, you think I've gone loony tunes, is that it? Well, my boy, I haven't. I'll tell you why. Because if I'm right about this monster, and I believe I am, the creature is repelled by facts. Terrified of the press! The legitimate press, I'm talking about. Here, catch!" He tossed me a copy of *The New York Times*. "Make a necklace out of Krugman's column and tie it around her neck. And you, Tarzan --" He began flinging magazines at Arthur like a peanut vendor at a ballpark – *The New Yorker, The Nation, Mother Jones*—one after the other. "Nail these to the wall above her bed in the shape of a cross!"

"Come on, Doc!" said Arthur in an exasperated tone. "What the hell? Bats can't read…"

"All will be revealed in time, my friend," said Bernie as he went about his work.

Arthur gave me a hopeless look. I shrugged at him. And so we did as Bernie suggested, though I could tell that Arthur was beginning to lose patience with the Professor, and I must confess, I felt distinctly like an idiot doing as he instructed. Soon, Miss Lucy's entire room was wreathed in newsprint. The Professor was quite picky about which newspapers and magazines were to be used. Only the legitimate press, he insisted. "None of that phony-baloney right-wing propaganda!" And he made sure all pages were turned to articles or columns about the new president, but only those stories that exposed his lies, or reported on his many controversies and failures, such as the growing scandal over his connections to vampires.

"The power of the press, my friends!" exclaimed Bernie. "Our enemy may have the millionaires and billionaires, but we have the fifth estate!"

Lucy woke up while we were covering her bed with newspapers. She began writhing and whimpering beneath her covers as if she were in the throes of a violent fever, then suddenly she bolted upright, her eyes open wide and wild-looking, her lips curling into a snarl. When she saw the newspapers lying atop her bedclothes, she hissed violently, and angrily swept them from the bed. "Lies!" she spat. "Fake news! It's nothing but lies!" Her voice seemed raspy and raw. Then she rose up on all fours like a cat, with her back in the air, and began crawling toward us with a wanton look on her pale, lovely face. I have to admit, she looked quite fetching, in a totally deranged, animalistic sort of way.

Poor Arthur flung himself to her on the bed, wrapped his arms around her and tried to comfort her. Lucy lay back on her pillows and began squirming in a most suggestive manner, smiling at her fiancée most voluptuously. "Ohh, Arthur," she cooed in a very sexy voice. "You're such a beast. Will you kiss me, Arthur?" And Holmwood, the poor fellow, could scarcely resist her, as fetching as she was, squirming away on the bed beneath him, and he, of course, being so much in love with her as he is. He bent eagerly to kiss her. Lucy's eyes widened as she rose to meet his lips. Then, just as they were about to meet, she turned her face to his neck and opened her mouth, and her teeth looked longer and sharper than any I have seen, particularly the canines, which, by some trick of the light, looked like the fangs of an animal.

At that instant, Van Helsing swooped upon Arthur, and, wrapping his arms around Holmwood's chest, and, with the strength of a much younger man, dragged him off of Lucy and hurled him from the bed. Lucy snarled at the Professor like a wildcat, but Bernie held his ground.

"No!" he yelled, pointing down at her. "Not on your life, missy! We have enormous problems facing this country, and I think we've got bigger things to worry about than your sex life! Like maybe we should raise the minimum wage, and maybe we should not be giving huge tax breaks to millionaires and billionaires! But I'll be damned if I'll let you spread the curse of the wampyre!"

I kept my eyes fixed on Lucy, as did we all in that room, and we saw a spasm of rage flit like a shadow over her face, the sharp teeth champed together. Then she suddenly seemed to grow tired again, her eyes closed, and she collapsed back onto the bed, asleep before her head hit the fluffy pillows.

DR. SEWARD'S DIARY

20th March, 2017 – Van Helsing left to go back to his home in Georgetown to retrieve what he called his "vampire kit" – a collection of special tools, he said, which he'd collected over the years and that we would need to fight and kill the bloodsucker. I assured the Professor that I would stand guard over Lucy, as Holmwood was dead on his feet and needed to rest after staying up with her the night before. So I settled down into the deep cushions of a comfortable chair beside Lucy's bed, with several of the Professor's magazines to keep me company.

Around eleven, my cellphone rang. It was one of the nurses from the asylum with most disturbing news. Apparently Seanfield had overpowered one of his attendants and run amok. He was hiding in my office, having locked the door, and was turning the place upside down. I had to go at once to calm the poor lunatic. As Holmwood was already sound asleep, I didn't want to wake him, so I called one of the asylum's off-duty nurses and asked if she wouldn't mind coming over to sit with Miss Lucy. Her name was Elsa, and she was a genial middle-aged woman who lived close by. She said she'd be happy to come, and could be there right away. Within fifteen minutes there was a knock at Lucy's front door and there she was. I pointed her to Lucy's room, and instructed that under no circumstances whatsoever was she to leave Lucy's side. Then off I bolted to deal with the maniac Seanfield.

Upon arrival at the asylum, I went directly upstairs to my office, where Seanfield had barricaded himself behind a locked door. I could see him through the small, square window in my door, dancing around my office in his tighty whities. I could hear him, too, calling out to his Master at the top of his lungs. "I serve you, Master! It is I, Seanfield. I live to serve you! Your wish is my command! Master!"

I unlocked the door with my key, but the lunatic had pushed my desk over, blocking the entrance. It took myself and three burly attendants several minutes to push it aside and gain entry. Then, once inside, we had to catch the squirrely bugger, who was now emptying my files and tossing the papers willy-nilly, whilst dashing across the room making strange animal noises. "Mooooo!" he bellowed like a mad cow. "Try and catch me, you dumb idiots!"

When at last we managed to apprehend the poor fool, he suddenly became quite placid, even genial, it seemed. As the attendants wrapped him tightly in a straitjacket, he smiled calmly at me and said in his squeaky voice, "Doctor Jack, it seems I've been rather naughty. Do not be angry with me. I have only done my Master's bidding. He has promised me eternal life." But as they led him back down to his padded room, he turned to the window and began hollering like a madman once again. "Are you pleased, Master? Have I pleased you? I am your slave! Master! Maaaster!"

I spent some time putting my office back together, then poured myself a Pimm's and drank it, enjoying the peace and quiet. It was nearly one a.m. by the time I went back out and climbed into my car for the drive back to Lucy's apartment.

All was dark and quiet as I turned down Lucy's street, and parked in front of her building. I went inside and rode the elevator up to the 11th floor, where Lucy's apartment occupied the northwest corner. I went in quietly, so as not to disturb Holmwood, who was snoring softly on the living room sofa. For an instant I paused at Lucy's bedroom door, not wanting to startle Elsa with too sudden an entrance, so I opened the door gently, and entered the room.

How can I describe what I saw? On the floor lay the nurse, covered in the newspapers that Van Helsing had so carefully placed on Lucy's windows and bed earlier. The window was flung open wide, the curtains billowing in the soft night breeze. On top of the bed, dressed only in her nightgown, lay Lucy, white arms stretched languidly above her head and dangling off the edge of the bed. Hunched over her was Trumpula, his cantaloupe colored face bent to the poor girl's neck, a whoosh of blond hair swooping forward across his forehead to cover Lucy's throat and the ghastly workings of his long, sharp teeth as he sucked the blood from her neck.

I let out an audible gasp. Startled, Trumpula raised his bloated orange face from Lucy's throat and hissed at me, his red eyes blazing like two burning embers. His face was a mask of pure hatred, blood dripping from his thin-lipped mouth.

I opened my mouth to speak, but all that came out were the words, "It's you!"

The Donald's features suddenly softened, his beady eyes changing back to a sparkling Prussian blue, his nectarine face relaxing into the natural Trumpula smirk I'd seen so many times on TV during the campaign, and before that, on his television show. He pursed his lips and raised his pudgy little money clutchers, making odd, circular movements with them as he spoke. "Wrong. It's not me. I was never here. I don't know Putin, have no deals in Russia, Russia is a ruse."

"My God," I said. "You… you're a vampire!"

"Fake news!" he hissed, pointing dramatically at me. "I'm not a vampire. You're a vampire. Apologize!"

I shook my head with disbelief. "What? I'm not going to apologize. You're a vampire. I just caught you sucking the blood from that poor girl's neck, which, the last time I checked, is pretty much the definition of the word 'vampire.' You've still got blood dripping from your fangs, for god's sake!"

Trumpula dabbed at the corner of his mouth with his sleeve. "I demand a retraction! Apologize!"

"You're insane. I'm not apologizing." I pointed at his lip. "You've still got a spot there… No, the other side…" I pointed to a drop of blood on the left side of his mouth.

He turned to Lucy's vanity, next to the bed, and bent over, peering into the mirror. "Where?" he said. "I don't see anything?"

"Of course you don't see anything. You're a bloody vampire, and you cast no reflection!"

He turned back to me, wiping at his puckered lips. Then pulled out his phone and began jabbing at it with his stubby fingers. "Ahh!" he said, smirking as he held the phone up at me. "Total vindication. Breitbart just published a headline that says, 'Trumpula is not a vampire.' Thank you, Breitbart. Will the mainstream media apologize? Many, many witnesses."

"You can forget about it," I said. "I'm not apologizing. I just caught you red-handed. Literally. You've got Lucy's blood on your hands from where you were biting her neck with your freakishly large fangs! Right there." I pointed at his tiny hand, which was dripping a steady stream of blood drops onto the carpet. He reached over and wiped it on Lucy's nightdress.

"You obviously get your news from the failing *New York Times*. You will soon apologize," he told me.

"No, I won't!" I said stubbornly, folding my arms.

He looked at his phone. "Wrong. You just sent me a really nice letter of apology." He looked up at me. "I don't accept. Loser."

"What?" I was really getting angry by this point. "I did no such thing! You're delusional!"

"I'm not delusional, you're delusional, and I don't accept

your apology, I'll never accept it so stop trying to apologize." He put his hand up, his soft, pink palm facing me in a stop sign.

My jaw dropped open and I stared at him, not believing my eyes, or ears.

"See you in court!" he spat, then drew his long, black cape over his face and disappeared in a vaporous mist. Then, out of the mist, a large bat with a poof of blond hair on its head flitted straight at me, squeaking loudly. I ducked, waving my arms wildly at the creature. The bat shrieked past me and flew out the window, just as Holmwood burst into the room.

"What the…" he cried. "Lucy!" He ran to the poor girl, who lay unconscious on the bed, her face as white as alabaster. The newspapers that had been tied round her neck and covered her bed were now strewn across the floor, lying all around the unconscious nurse. Holmwood wrapped Lucy in his arms and lifted her limp body, calling her name over and over. I could see, on her bare throat, the two little wounds, now looking horribly white and mangled, and rimmed red with blood.

The physician in me suddenly took over and I stepped quickly toward the bed. Taking Lucy's wrist in my hand, I felt for a pulse. Her skin was ice cold to the touch, and she did not appear to be breathing. I could detect no pulse, and I realized I never would.

Arthur looked at me. "Jack?" he asked me, his voice cracking with emotion. "Is she…"

I nodded, and placed my hand upon his shoulder. "It is all over," I told him solemnly. "She is dead."

COUNT TRUMPULA'S TWITTER ACCOUNT

Donald J. Trumpula@RealTrumpula 21st March, 2017, 3:13 a.m.

Dopey, failed Dr. Seward called me a vampire. Major loser. Zero credibility. Another win for Trumpula! #MASA

JONATHAN HARKER'S JOURNAL

22nd March, 2017 – What a terrible shock for my dear Mimi, indeed for all of us, as we awoke early yesterday to the news that Mimi's best friend in all the world, sweet, beautiful Lucy, has died. Mimi is inconsolable. She blames herself, as if she should have somehow seen the future, and come home sooner, or dashed over to see Lucy as soon as we arrived from Florida last night. I'm afraid my ordeal has been quite draining for Mimi, having to spend weeks in my hospital room, waiting on me hand and foot, only to finally come home to this dreadful news. She remains in bed, too overcome with grief to even get up and dress. She has asked me to go and fetch Kat from Lucy's apartment, which, of course, I am glad to do, as I know the little furball will help Mimi smile again.

I got up and put on a pot of coffee. The newspaper outside our apartment door blared the day's headline at me from the Welcome mat:

"TRUMPULA ISSUES TRAVEL BAN BANNING VAMPIRE HUNTERS"

I took the paper inside, poured a cup of java, then sat down at the kitchen table and read the article.

"President Trumpula signed an executive order Sunday to keep foreign vampire hunters from seven countries from entering the U.S. The countries affected are Transylvania, Bulgaria, Rumania, Walachia, Moldavia, Bukovina, and Hungaria.

The ban caused widespread confusion at airports around the country, as airport security officials were told to stop and detain anyone from the seven Eastern European nations suspected of being a "vampire hunter, vampire killer, or vampire slayer."

The ban snared green card holders and people with valid visas alike. Anyone traveling with a crucifix, garlic, wooden sticks that could be sharpened into stakes, wafers or "holy water," were affected. Some travelers who were in the air when Trumpula signed the order weren't able to enter the country when they landed. Some were detained. Others were sent back to where they flew in from. By early Sunday evening, massive protests had erupted at airports around the world.

In a statement, the White House described Count Trumpula's directive as "lawful and appropriate."

"The President's order is intended to protect the homeland," read the statement, "and he has the constitutional authority and responsibility to protect the American people from these stake-pounding, cross-clutching fanatics."

I folded the paper and turned on the news on the TV. It seemed a federal judge had already issued an emergency stay of the travel ban against vampire hunters, and the President was livid. But I wasn't prepared for the intensity of my feelings when they cut to the Count speaking from the White House. When I saw his bloated, venomous face, it brought the entire, terrible Mar-a-Lago ordeal back to me in vivid color, and I dropped my cup, spilling coffee all over the floor.

MIMI MURRAY'S JOURNAL

22nd March, 2017—I heard a crash in the other room and got up to investigate. I found Jonathan staring at the TV, muttering to himself, his coffee cup in pieces on the parquet floor, with a small pool of spilled coffee at his feet. I didn't care. It was just a cup. I put my arms around him, hugging him close, and laid my head on his broad shoulder, and he put his hands on mine, squeezing. But he clutched my wrist so tightly that he hurt me, and I heard him whisper, "My God!" I lifted my head and looked at him, but his eyes were locked on the television.

"Look, Mimi!" he said, pointing at the TV. "Look at him!"

I turned to the TV. Trumpula was on the screen, blathering about something with his ridiculous third-grade vocabulary. With the TV on mute, I couldn't tell what he was talking about, and I didn't care, but Jonathan seemed very distressed.

"It is the man himself," he said, his face growing pale. "It's him—the Count! He looks different somehow. Younger. Oh, God, that's it! He looks as if he's grown young!"

He aimed the remote at the screen and turned the volume up. Der Pumpkinfuhrer was bloviating to his blank-faced faithful, making small circles in the air with his tiny pink pussy pinchers, as if he were polishing an invisible window.

"They can't stand it because we suck," he gloated, a despicably smug expression on his pompous cheeseball face. "But we're going to keep on sucking, believe me. We're going to suck so much you're going to get tired of sucking, you're going to say, 'Please, Mr. President, I have a headache. Please, don't suck so much. This is getting terrible.' And I'm going to say, 'No, we have to make America suck again!' You're gonna say, 'Please.' I'm gonna say, 'Nope. Nope. We're gonna keep sucking.'"

The small crowd went wild, chanting "USA! USA!" in mindless unison. Some raised their arms, reaching out for their orange Jesus, crying, "Master! Master!" Still others made the Nazi salute, right there in broad daylight. Trumpula smirked and nodded as he gazed at his hypnotized minions. I shuddered, snatched the remote from Jonathan's hand and clicked off the TV. "Come on," I told him. "Let's go get Kat."

He looked up at me as if he were lost in a trance and didn't know who I was. But then he shook his head, clearing whatever cobwebs were fogging his mind. "But I thought you weren't up to going?" he said.

"I changed my mind," I told him. "Go get dressed."

COUNT TRUMPULA'S TWITTER ACCOUNT

Donald J. Trumpula@RealTrumpula 22nd March, 2017, 4:04 a.m.

I have instructed Homeland Security to check people coming into our country with garlic and wooden stakes VERY CAREFULY.

Donald J. Trumpula@RealTrumpula 22nd March, 2017, 4:06 a.m.

Everybody is arguing whether or not it is a BAN. Call it what you want, it's about keeping bad people (with wooden stakes) out of country!

Donald J. Trumpula@RealTrumpula 22nd March, 2017, 4:10 a.m.

MAKE AMERICA SUCK AGAIN! #AmericaThirst

Donald J. Trumpula@RealTrumpula 22nd March, 2017, 6:39 a.m.

This ruling makes us look weak, which by the way we no longer are, believe me! We're going to fight this terrible ruling.

Donald J. Trumpula@RealTrumpula 22nd March, 2017, 6:40 a.m.

Cannot believe a judge would put our country in such peril. If something happens, blame him and courts. Vampire killers pouring in. Bad!

Donald J. Trumpula@RealTrumpula 22nd March, 2017, 6:45 a.m.

We must keep dangerous vampire "hunters" out of our country! #MASA

MIMI MURRAY'S JOURNAL

22nd March, 2017 – We went to Lucy's apartment to pick up Kat. Dr. Seward was there with Arthur, trying to put things in order, but poor Arthur could barely speak. Dr. Seward gave him a sleeping pill and he went into Lucy's room and lay down on the bed. I feel so badly for him, the poor fellow, he truly, truly loved Lucy.

I took Dr. Seward aside and asked him to tell me what happened, and he told us the whole horrific story.

Under normal circumstances, it would all seem ridiculous, even comical—Trumpula a vampire. Sweet zombie Jesus, the President, an actual vampire! A greedy, perfidious, pussy-grabbing chiseler? Yes. An abominable, baby-fingered, tangerine-faced, fascist? Absolutely. But a vampire? Vampires, I mean real, honest-to-goodness, undead, cape-wearing, coffin-dwelling neck-suckers, they don't really exist, right? That's what I thought, too, up until a couple of weeks ago, back before Jonathan's experience with the Melon-Faced Monster of Mar-a-Lago. But now, now my best friend is dead, and my fiancée nearly dead on account of this tangerine fiend. We must do something! Dr. Seward says that his friend, Professor Van Helsing, seems to know a lot about vampires, and how to fight them. I am anxious to meet him. If what he says is true, I want to make that evil, failed mail-order meat salesman pay! I want to be the one to personally drive a stake through his shriveled black heart and watch him die. Die slowly and painfully, a hideous, horrible, torturous, mutilated, writhing, screaming, blood-puking, shit-stinking death. A death so terrible and horrifying that most people will feel sorry for the orange-tufted imbecile. But not me. I'll be too busy dancing on his grave. Die, monster, die!

DR. SEWARD'S DIARY

27th March, 2017 – Lucy's funeral has been set for tomorrow. Her best friend, Mimi, has been attending to all the ghastly formalities. She is a rock, and her fiancée, John Harker, is a very lucky fellow indeed. Holmwood tries to help, but he is an emotional wreck, totally and utterly devastated by the loss of his dear Lucy, and who can blame him? Harker is still recovering from his own ordeal with the Count. Lucy's sister, parents, grandparents, and extended family, also are in shock and grieving. So it falls to Mimi. Dealing with the coroner to get Lucy's body, arranging the undertaker and the casket and the funeral and her funeral clothes, a viewing at the mortician's, a wake for her and Lucy's friends and coworkers from the Library, on and on. All of this and more Mimi takes upon herself. She is tireless and driven, and more than anything she wants revenge for the one who took her dearest friend from her in such a cruel fashion. And unless I miss my guess, she plans to get it.

Meanwhile, Van Helsing is busy making plans of his

own. He carries what he calls his "vampire kit" with him at all times now. How he manages it I haven't a clue – the thing must weigh four stone! It is an ancient, weather-beaten, leather doctor's bag, containing a number of mysterious and surprising items, which the Professor explained were carefully chosen specifically to do battle with Count Trumpula. For instance, instead of a crucifix, which is a mainstay for most vampire kits, Van Helsing's Trumpula kit contains a Rosie O'Donnell Friend of Barbie Barbie Doll. Instead of a Bible, there is a Pocket Edition of the U.S. Constitution (including the Bill of Rights). Rather than little glass vials of blessed Holy Water, there are little glass vials of Trumpula Vodka, which, the Professor assures us, tastes like Russian feet. Instead of cloves of garlic, there are bundles of cannibis. In addition to wooden stakes, there are several Trumpula steaks, frozen slabs of beef cut so that long, sharpened bones stick out at the ends. They also taste like Russian feet. And instead of holy communion wafers, there are piles of hard-shell corn tortillas carried personally across the border from Mexico by immigrants. There is also a boombox with a CD player, a compact disc of Cher's Greatest Hits, and an iPad with a high-speed wireless Internet connection, loaded with bookmarks to snopes.com and factcheck.org, as well as digital copies of *Michael Moore in Trumpland*, and the collected works of Meryl Streep.

THE NOTES OF DONALD J. TRUMPULA AS RECORDED ON OBAMA'S SECRET WIRETAPP SURVEILLANCE SYSTEM

27th March, 2017 – Hello, Barack. It's me again, The Donald, 45th President of the United States. I'm here to record Chapter Five of my memoir on your secret wiretapp. The continuation of "Bite Me: Donald J. Trumpula's Life as the Greatest Vampire President Ever in the History of the Universe. PERIOD!" by Count Donald J. Trumpula.

Chapter 6. The 1950s and 60s. In the 1950s, you had Senator Joe McCarthy, who was a really great guy, did an amazing job. He identified many, many communists working for Russia against our country's interests. Put a lot of them in jail, and really just made America great again. I didn't testify before his commission, the Committee on Un-American Activities, but I would have loved to testify. Would have loved to name names, and believe me, I had a lot of names. The best names. I could have filled a notebook with the names I had, trust me. And I would have testified, but I had a doctor that gave me a very strong letter on the heels. So I couldn't testify, obviously, I had the thing with the heels. Anyway, the 50s were great. Everyone knew their place. The blacks knew their place, the women, the gays. Everyone knew, and it was great. Until the '60s came along, and things got very, very complicated. You had the whole Civil Rights movement, with Dr. Martin Luther King, and they just stirred up a lot of bad blood. A lot of confusion. And he was no doctor, believe me, this guy, King. An extremely credible source called my office and told me that Martin Luther King was not a real doctor. He said he ran into so-called "Doctor" King and asked him about his lumbago, asked him to take a look at it, and King had no clue what he was talking about. So I said to myself, 'what kind of a doctor could he be?' So I went on Huntley and Brinkley on NBC and I said, "If he's really a doctor, why doesn't he show us his medical certificate? I'll tell you, I have people that actually have been studying it, and they cannot believe what they're finding. At some point, when the time is right, I'll be releasing the results of my investigation, and a lot of people will be very impressed, believe me." And the best part is, Huntley and Brinkley got the best ratings they ever had for that show. Number one, thanks to me.

But the '60s weren't all bad. You had free love. I enjoyed myself very, very heavily. Then came the Vietnam War. I was never a fan of the Vietnam War, but I was never at the protest level either, because I had other things to do. Like playing golf, moving very heavily on girls, biting people, that kind of thing. But I had a doctor that gave me a letter – a very strong letter on the heels. And I had a very high draft number, phenomenal number. I was going to the Wharton School of Business, and I was watching as they did the draft numbers. This was 1968, 1969. And I remember, Teddy was there. Ted Nugent, and boy did he stink. He'd soiled himself a few days before to get out of the draft and he was just walking around like that for days. Sad. But that was Vietnam. I'll never forget, that was an amazing period of time in my life. Avoiding sexually transmitted diseases while dating, that was my personal Vietnam.

But I sacrificed. I think I made a lot of sacrifices. I work very, very hard, created thousands and thousands of jobs, built great structures. I've had tremendous success. I've made a lot of money. I think I've done a lot. Played a lot of golf, grabbed a lot of women by the bum fiddle, which is what we used to call it back in the 17th century. And now I'm President. And you're not.

LUCY WESTENRA'S TWITTER ACCOUNT

Lucy Westenra@lucygoosy 27th March, 2017, 10:20 p.m.

For the first time in history people are angry with a politician for keeping his campaign promises. MAKE AMERICA SUCK AGAIN! #TRUMPULA 2020

Lucy Westenra@lucygoosy 27th March, 2017, 10:26 p.m.

America First! Trumpula's Budget Slashes Foreign Aid by 28 Percent! We cannot afford to keep bailing out the whole world! MASA.

Lucy Westenra@lucygoosy 27th March, 2017, 10:33 p.m.

WE LOVE OUR PRESIDENT! MASA.

Lucy Westenra@lucygoosy 27th March, 2017, 10:37 p.m.

Stop crying, Snowflakes!! The election is over!!!!!!!

Lucy Westenra@lucygoosy 27th March, 2017, 10:37 p.m.

Meals on Wheels is showing no results, so why keep spending $$$$? No more free sh*t, liberals! MASA!

MIMI MURRAY'S DIARY

27th March, 2017 – Dear Diary, soooo this happened: I just found out my dead friend Lucy is tweeting from the grave. No really. I went to Twitter and found a bunch of brand new tweets from Lucy. And all of them – every last single one— are totally freaking crazy-ass loony tunes off the cliff right-wing political bullshart in support of Trumpula. Which Lucy would never do, as in NEVEREVEREVEREVER! Ever!!! She hated Orange Hitler! WTAF!?! Someone has obviously hacked her account, right? Has to be! But why now? So then I go to Facebook and guess what? Yep. Same thing. All these posts from Lucy 4 days after she died saying what a great prez Trumpula is, and "Make America Suck Again" this and "Make America Suck Again" that. Grrr!

So I called Lucy's sister Charlotte to tell her and she said her whole family had just found her Facebook posts and were freaking out! Whoever's doing this needs to rot in hell for all eternity. It's beyond cruel.

DR. SEWARD'S DIARY

28th March, 2017 – Yesterday the undertaker held the viewing of the body. Holmwood was there, and Lucy's family, and Harker and Mimi, of course, and many other friends of Lucy's from the Library and her school days. Van Helsing came, too, bounding into the place in his rumpled suit, carrying his monstrous vampire kit, his hair looking as if it had been combed with a lint roller. He came charging up to the crowd gathered round Lucy's coffin, with the poor girl lying there looking so peaceful and lovely. Indeed, she makes a very beautiful corpse; death has given her back her loveliness, and her cheeks have got their colour back, and her beautiful face has regained all of its allure. The Westenras are a very old Washington family, dating back to colonial days, and quite well off, from what I've been told, and they've spared no expense with the undertaking.

Bernie bent over the coffin, looking closely at her, so close his face was nearly touching Lucy's, and I saw him pulling the collar of her dress back from her neck, as if he were inspecting the body for something. Then, rising, he said to me, "Look, Jack, look at her throat!"

I bent over and peered closely at Lucy's neck, as the Professor pulled back the dress so that I could see. And I did see. The wounds on her throat had completely disappeared. I looked at Bernie. "The undertaker is first rate," I whispered.

Bernie shook his head gravely, then put his fingers on Lucy's neck where the puncture wounds had once been. "See?" he said, rubbing her throat vigorously. "The wounds are gone!"

I frowned at him. "But what does it mean?"

Before he had a chance to answer, someone behind us said, "Poor girl, at least her pain is at an end. She's at peace now."

Bernie bolted upright, whirling around to face the crowd of mourners standing there. "Sadly," he said, "no. She is not at peace. Not yet. And, unfortunately, this is not the end of our dear Lucy's suffering. Indeed, though it pains me to say it, this is just the beginning."

Lucy's poor mother, standing there in the crowd that included Lucy's father and sister and several others, was taken aback. "What do you mean?" she asked, her voice throbbing with outrage.

Bernie just shook his head and said, "Well, I mean that, if we want to save poor Lucy's soul, there is much work to be done, folks." While the crowd murmured with confusion, Van Helsing continued. "Mr. and Mrs. Westenra, tomorrow, after the funeral, but before the burial, I'd like your permission to spend some time alone with Lucy's corpse."

Lucy's mother gasped, her father turned beet red and took a step toward Bernie, and Arthur's eyes bulged from their sockets. "Good God, man," I said, grabbing the Professor's elbow. "What on earth are you on about?"

Bernie clapped his hands together. "Well now, it'll only take a few minutes, but before sundown tomorrow, I need to drive a stake through Lucy's heart, cut off her head and stuff her mouth with holy wafers. Otherwise, she'll be condemned for all eternity to stalk the living as one of the undead, an insatiable blood-sucking vampire. I think we can all agree, that is unacceptable, and that has got to change…"

Lucy's mother let out a high-pitched shriek, threw her glass of water in the Professor's face and then fainted dead away to the floor, her father grabbed Bernie in a headlock and began pummeling him with short jabs to the top of his bald head, while her sister set about kicking the Professor's shins. Harker and I tried to stop them, and, eventually, we were able to pry the old man off of Bernie. I took Van Helsing into the restroom, away from the angry crowd, so he could clean up and I could have a word.

"Was it something I said, Jack?" he asked incredulously, dabbing blood from his lip with a handkerchief.

"Something?" I yelled. "No, Professor. It was everything! Why in God's name would you wish to speak of mutilating that poor, beautiful girl like that, in front of all her family and friends?"

Bernie turned towards me, his shoulders hunched up around his ears, and he began jabbing his finger as if he were writing in the air without a pen. "Jack, my boy, you were there. You saw what happened to Lucy with your own eyes. Trumpula sucked the very life out of that poor girl. He killed her, but she's not dead. She is nosferatu, the undead. Now, we got two choices here. Either we can lay down and surrender, and let the Trumpulas of the world, these billionaire bloodsuckers, ride roughshod over the people, or we stand up and say, 'enough is enough!' We fight back! And I, for one, am not about to see that poor, beautiful girl be turned into a vile bloodsucking demon from Hell! I say tomorrow, after her funeral, we go down there, pry her coffin open, and do whatever is necessary to set her free from that creature's evil spell. And then, when that disgusting job is done, we must seek out Trumpula himself in his lair and destroy him. Now, are you with me?"

I stared at him, an empty feeling in the pit of my stomach, but my mind flashed back to the dreadful scene in Lucy's bedroom the night of her death, Trumpula defiling her on her bed and sucking her blood. I nodded my approval. "Yes, Professor," I said. "I'm with you."

Just then there was the sound of a toilet flushing from one of the stalls behind us. We watched in the mirror as the door to the stall opened and out stepped Mimi, a look of utter determination and anger on her lovely face. Her heels made loud clicks on the tile as she walked toward us. We stared at her, our mouths agape as she stepped calmly to the sink between us. "So am I," she said, turning on the faucet and pressing soap out of the dispenser. She looked directly at Bernie as she washed. "Count me in, Professor. Let's kick Hair Fuhrer's orange bloodsucking ass!"

As she took a paper towel from the dispenser and dried her hands, Bernie said, "Thank you, Mimi. But are you sure you're up for this? This Trumpula is a monster. He's strong, powerful, determined, and capable of committing monstrous acts, as we have seen."

Mimi squashed the towel into a little ball and spiked it into the garbage can below the sink. "Professor," she said, with a steely look in her eyes, "That pumpkin-faced fucker killed my best friend and tried to kill my fiancée. I'm a public librarian. A woman of information. I'm the thing that monsters like him have nightmares about."

She walked to the door and opened it, then paused, turning back to us. "Oh, and FYI..." She pointed her thumb at the figure of a girl on the door. "You're in the ladies' room. Professor."

JONATHAN HARKER'S DIARY

28th March, 2017 – After the viewing, Mimi, Holmwood, and I were approached by Van Helsing and Dr. Seward, who asked that we join them tomorrow night, after the burial, at Lucy's gravesite, for what he called a "mission."

"What kind of mission?" asked Holmwood, skeptically.

"My boy," said the Professor, "it is a mission of mercy, indeed, for poor Lucy is not at peace. She is not free."

"Professor," said Arthur in an exasperated tone. "Please stop being so cryptic and tell me the truth. What do you mean by, 'not free'? Is this more of your vampire nonsense, because if it is, I warn you…"

Van Helsing peered through his glasses at Arthur. Clearly he could see what we all could: that Arthur was at the end of his tether, still devastated by the loss of his fiancée and not in the mood for any shenanigans.

"All right, Mr. Holmwood," said Bernie, poking his finger at the air. "Here's what I mean. People are not truly free when they're unable to feed their family. People are not truly free when they're unable to retire with dignity. People are not truly free when they're unemployed or underemployed, or when they have no health care. And people are certainly not free when they've been bitten by a blood-sucking vampire, not even after they're dead. Because they're not truly dead, Mr. Holmwood. They're undead. And that's the state that Lucy is in right now. Undead. Which is about 65 percent dead, 35 percent not dead, according to my calculations. Condemned to live forever as a blood-sucker herself, rising from her grave at night to haunt the living, much like student loans haunt college students for decades after graduation. Unless we free her. And, Arthur, if you love that girl, and I know that you do, you'll want to free her, believe me."

Holmwood's face gradually turned redder as the

Professor spoke, until it seemed as if he were about to explode and throttle the old fellow. Then Dr. Seward stepped forward and put his arm on Arthur's shoulder.

"Arthur," he said. "Everything the Professor has told you is true. I saw it. The night of Lucy's death, she was attacked by... by a vampire. I saw him. He was on top of her on the bed, sucking the blood from her neck. Then he turned into a bat and flew out the window before you burst into the room. I know how ridiculous it sounds, but it's true. Every word of it, I swear it."

Arthur stared at him in disbelief. His gaze traveled from Dr. Seward to myself to Mimi. Seeing that we all believed what Dr. Seward had told him, he collapsed into a chair and buried his face in his hands. "I can't believe it," he said.

Seward sat in the chair beside him and put his arm around the poor man. "I never would have believed it myself," he said soothingly, "if I hadn't seen it with my own eyes."

Arthur looked up at us through misty eyes. "Mimi? Jonathan? You believe this?"

Mimi nodded and took my hand. "Yes. Yes we do." Then, looking at me, she said, "Tell him, Jonathan. Tell him about Mar-a-Lago."

I took a deep breath, for those dreadful events still weighed heavily on my mind. "I wouldn't have believed it, either, Arthur," I said, softly. "Until my experience at Mar-a-Lago. But I saw things there I never would have thought possible. Yes, Arthur, I'm afraid it's true. The Professor's right. Lucy was the victim of a vampire."

"Not 'was,' Jonathan," said the Professor. "Is still. She *is* the victim of a vampire, I'm afraid. Once you are bitten by the wampyr, you become a wampyr, unless the wampyr who bit you is destroyed before you turn, which only happens in about 6 percent of all cases. It's pretty complicated, but trust me. The way it works is like this: the boss vampire bites some poor schmuck, who then becomes a vampire himself. Then he goes around biting people, and turning them. And then those schmucks turn, and bite more people. It's a vicious circle. Like the big banks, too big to fail. We must break up Big Vampire! And the only way to do that is to kill the head nosferatu. Or as I like to call him, the bossferatu."

"But how?" said Arthur. "We don't even know who he is!"

"Oh yes we do," said Bernie. "Prepare yourselves for a shock. It's Trumpula!"

"Psshhh," said Holmwood, thinking the Professor must be joking, but then quickly realized he was not. "You mean... the President?"

"One and the same," said Bernie.

"But that's preposterous!" said Arthur. "You can't be serious!"

"I'm serious as satellite radio," said the Professor. "Let's look at the evidence, shall we? Number one. Lucy became ill just after the inauguration, which is right when the Count came to Washington. Number two. That is also the same time that your unfortunate patient, Mister Seanfield, arrived at your asylum, Jack, raving that his Master was at hand to, quote, make America suck again, unquote. And, number three, his Master brought him a Make America Suck Again cap, just like the kind worn by Trumpula's supporters. Number four. In Lucy's recurring nightmare, she described being attacked by a vulgar, orange-skinned man with blond, swirly hair. Who does that sound like?"

Dr. Seward raised his hand. "Also, I saw the vampire actually in the act of biting Lucy, and it was Trumpula, no question about it. I even spoke with him. It was him. I'd swear it on a stack of bibles. So, there's that."

Van Helsing put both hands on Arthur's shoulders and shook him. "Now do you believe us, Arthur? Count Trumpula is a vampire. A narsferatu."

"You mean NOS-feratu, don't you?" said Seward.

Bernie let Arthur go and stood up straight to face the doctor. "No, Jack. He is Narsferatu. The narcissistic vampire."

"Well what are we waiting for?" said Mimi. "Let's go kill the orange fucker!"

"Wait," said Bernie. "First things first. This vampire we fight, this one we face, Trumpula, he is no ordinary wampyr. No, he is their leader! And he is very powerful. We must prepare and plan before we take him on. But first we must take care of our dear friend, Lucy, who remains in his thrall. We must go, tomorrow night, after the funeral, and we must free her. So come, my friends, for there is much planning and work, wild work to be done!"

COUNT TRUMPULA'S TWITTER ACCOUNT

Donald J. Trumpula@RealTrumpula 29th March, 2017, 4:04 a.m.

This Vampire investigation is a witch hunt by media & Dems of historic proportions! Very unfair to Trumpula!

MIMI MURRAY'S JOURNAL

29th March, 2017 – I only need two words to describe Van Helsing: Kick. Ass! He has his old man moments, and his old man bed hair, which is high-larious. He looks like a villain who gets unmasked at the end of Scooby Doo. But when it comes to vampires, the dude knows his stuff.

So after his little pep talk to Arthur, the Professor asked Jonathan if he would tell him, in detail, everything about his time with the Count at Mar-a-Lago, so that he could learn all that he possibly could about Trumpula, and how to beat him. I think Jonathan was, at first, a bit hesitant, but I say if it helps us kick some bloodsucker butt, I'm all for it. I asked Jonathan if he would do it for Lucy, and Jonathan agreed. So we went back to our apartment and Jonathan spent the next couple of hours telling him the whole story, soup to nuts. Everything, from the moment he arrived in West Palm Beach and the gypsy lady warned him, to finding Trumpula in the tanning bed/coffin, to the Russian pee hookers and Jonathan's eventual escape. Then I told the Professor about Jonathan's journal, and convinced Johnny to let the Professor read the entries he wrote from Mar-a-Lago.

When the professor finished reading, he said nothing, just closed the notebook, stood up and walked over to Jonathan and asked to shake his hand. "You, sir, are a very brave man," he told him. Jonathan opened his mouth but nothing came out, and then he started to choke up and the tears started streaming down his face. It was honestly as emotional as I've ever seen Jonathan. The Professor gave him a big hug and tears were coming down his cheeks, too, and the whole thing was so damn touching that I started crying too. I think we were all thinking about Lucy, and also what Jonathan went through at the runty hands of Nectarine Idi Amin, and it all just came spilling out.

Finally, after the three of us had shared a good cry, we dried our eyes and Bernie started waving his arms above his shoulders like The Flying Nun coming in for a landing. "I'll tell you one thing right now, John and Mimi," he said. "We're going to win. You know how I know that? Because I know that when we stand together and fight back against the powerful special interests, when we say enough is enough, we won't accept racism, we won't accept sexism, we won't accept vampirism, when we stand together, there is nothing we can't accomplish." Then he told us to get a good night's sleep, because we would surely need it tomorrow, and he left.

DR. SEWARD'S DIARY

30th March, 2017 – It was nearing midnight when the five of us arrived at the cemetery where the Westenra family vault was located – Van Helsing, Holmwood, Harker, Mimi, and myself. The night was dark, with occasional gleams of moonlight as the full moon danced among the heavy clouds that scudded across the sky. Using the sporadic moonlight and the beams from the flashlights the Professor had provided to us, we made our way through the tombstones to Lucy's crypt. Holmwood had the key, and he opened the creaky door to the crypt, then stood back, allowing the Professor to enter first. One by one, we entered the vault behind him, and set our flashlights around the outer edges of the crypt, pointing up so the light would reflect off the vault's ceiling and illuminate the room sufficiently for the Professor to do his "wild work," as he called it.

Lucy's coffin was in the center of the crypt. Van Helsing moved to the head of the casket and took a crowbar from inside his kit and pried off the lid. It took all five of us to slide the extremely heavy top off the coffin. I heard a hiss escape Van Helsing's lips, and we all crowded 'round and looked inside the box. The coffin was empty!

"My God," I said. "Where is she?"

"We are too late," said Van Helsing. "She walks among the living."

"Oh, come on!" spat Holmwood. "You can't seriously believe that!"

"What else?" said Van Helsing.

"I don't know," said Arthur. "Grave robbers?"

Bernie looked at him with a bemused expression on his face. "And how did they get in, Arthur? You have the key. There was no sign of forced entry. No, I'm afraid she has begun her career as a vampire."

"So what do we do now?" said Mimi.

"We wait," said Bernie. "Outside."

We slid the coffin lid back into place, retrieved our flashlights and left the tomb, each of us taking up a hiding spot behind the gravestones surrounding Lucy's crypt.

It was a lonely vigil, dank and chilly and very creepy, with the full moon playing hide and seek behind the clouds. The minutes crept by like Sisyphus pushing his giant rock. It was about three a.m. with the clouds suddenly parting like a curtain from the stage, leaving the sky to the white-bright moon, when I saw her, just a glimpse of white moving through the darkness at the bottom of the graveyard. I nudged Van Helsing and pointed at the ghostly figure in white that seemed to glide slowly through the headstones as it moved toward us. As the figure came closer, I could tell it was Lucy. She looked like a ghostly bride, wearing the same white dress she was buried in, and, oddly, what looked to be a bright red baseball-style hat atop her head, with the brim pulled down tight over her forehead. Van Helsing motioned for us all to remain hidden. When Lucy was no more than ten feet from the entrance to her tomb, Van Helsing suddenly rose from his hiding spot, brandishing a flashlight, which he aimed directly at Lucy's face, showering her with light. It was then that she turned, and the curious cap she wore upon her head was revealed in the moonlight and clear burst of Van Helsing's flash; it was the familiar red ballcap with a picture of white fangs and block letters across the front that read, "MAKE AMERICA SUCK AGAIN." But where had that come from? Had one of her family members – or perhaps one of the cemetery employees – a Trumpula supporter—placed it upon her head after the funeral? As the beam from Bernie's flashlight bathed Lucy's face in its white glow, she let out a loud hiss, revealing her long, sharp teeth. The rest of us stepped out from our hiding places then and shone our flashlights on Lucy too. Lucy drew back from us with an angry snarl, like a cat taken by surprise, as five shafts of light crisscrossed her face and bore into her burning red eyes. Her thin white arms tried to shield her face, moving in a creepy herky-jerky fashion, as if she were some hideous wind-up toy from hell. We advanced slowly, flashlights scorching her with light, forcing Lucy to retreat back towards her crypt.

Arthur, unable to contain himself any longer, let out a mournful moan. "Lucy!" he wailed.

Lucy dropped her arms from her eyes, her face wreathed with a voluptuous smile. "Come to me, Arthur. Leave these losers and come to me. My arms are hungry for you, my love. Come, and we can win together! Aren't you tired of losing, my love? Come with me and we will win so much you'll get tired of winning! You'll beg me: 'Lucy, Lucy, let me rest! I'm tired of winning!' And I'll say, 'No, Arthur, we have to make America suck again! We're going to keep winning.' Come, my love, come!"

"Crap on a spatula!" said Mimi. "She even sounds like Trumpula!"

Arthur seemed to fall under a spell as he moved toward her, opening his arms to his fiancée. Lucy lept for them, her cruel mouth opening wide, revealing the sharpened fangs ready to bite. And it was Van Helsing who saved him. He sprang forward, arms outstretched, thrusting the Rosie O'Donnell Barbie Doll in Lucy's face. She recoiled from it, hissing, her suddenly distorted features full of rage. Her red eyes blazed with an unholy light, and she covered her face with her skinny arms and the sleeves of her long dress as she turned towards her crypt. She moved sideways toward the entrance of her tomb in that odd, spasmodic fashion, as if she were a puppet on string commanded by some unseen hand, and then she went inside, slinking into the vault. Holmwood let out a terrible wailing cry, and then sunk to his knees, whimpering, as Mimi bent to comfort him.

Van Helsing, meanwhile, followed Lucy into the crypt, holding the Rosie doll before him, with myself and Harker right behind him.

As I entered the tomb behind the Professor, I saw Lucy climb into her coffin, her limbs moving in that same herky-jerky fashion. She lay down on her back, as if she were going to sleep. I watched as her thin, pale fingers slithered around the coffin lid, and she somehow moved back into place by herself that which it had taken five of us to remove. Van Helsing set his vampire kit down on the granite floor and opened it. Reaching inside, he pulled out one of his frozen Trumpula steaks with the long, sharpened bone protruding, and a heavy-duty sledgehammer. Then, as Mimi and Holmwood entered the tomb, Bernie motioned to the rest of us, and we surrounded the coffin. With each of us grabbing the heavy lid, we began to lift and slide it off the top of Lucy's coffin.

There lay Lucy, eyes closed, as if she were asleep in her bed. She was, if possible, more radiantly beautiful than ever. I found myself doubting for a moment that she was really dead. Her lips were red, and on her cheeks was a delicate bloom.

Van Helsing glanced at us, and the four of us lifted our flashlights to the coffin, shining fully on the creature inside that had once been Lucy. The Professor then placed the frozen steak directly over Lucy's heart, with the sharpened bone pointed down. Then, raising the heavy mallet, he shouted out, "Feel the Bern!" and swung. There was the sharp, reverberating sound of the hammer hitting the frozen steak, followed immediately by an awful squishing sound as the steakbone pierced Lucy's breast, and a spray of blood and other disgusting fluids came bursting out of her, splashing over our faces and clothing. The thing in the coffin awoke, its eyes bursting open as if to bulge out of her face, a hideous, blood-curdling screech escaping her curling, red lips. She writhed, her body convulsing and twisting in wild contortions; the sharp white teeth champing together till her lips were cut, and her mouth was smeared with a crimson foam. But the Professor never faltered. He looked like a figure of Thor pounding his mighty hammer as his untrembling arm rose and fell, hollering out "Feel the Bern!" with each stroke as he drove the steak deeper and deeper into Lucy's squirming body. And then the writhing and quivering of the body became less, and the teeth ceased to champ, and the face to quiver. Finally it lay still, and the terrible task was over. Well, almost.

The sledgehammer fell from Bernie's hand. He reeled back and would have fallen had we not caught him. Sweat was pouring from his bald forehead, and his glasses were so fogged that I wondered how he could see at all. He then bent to his kit and took out a short-handled axe. Lifting it to his shoulder, he strode to the head of the open coffin like a lumberjack. "Stand back," he said, glancing at the rest of us. And, as we stepped back from the coffin, he raised the ax above his head and with one mighty swing chopped Lucy's head from her shoulders.

"Oh, God!" gasped Arthur, as he fell back against the wall of the crypt.

Bernie dropped the axe then, with a loud clanging sound that echoed throughout the tomb. "Hand me a couple of those tortillas, will you Jack?" he asked me, pointing at his bag. I knelt down and rummaged through the kit until I found a plastic baggie full of hard-shelled corn tortillas, and I handed them to the Professor. Bernie took them and, leaning down into the coffin, began breaking them, one at a time, into smaller pieces and then stuffing the pieces into the open mouth of Lucy's severed head. Then he took from his kit a small vial of Trumpula Vodka and a copy of the United States Constitution, which he opened to the Bill of Rights. Standing fully erect over Lucy's beheaded, steak-pierced corpse, Van Helsing held the book in one hand, reciting from the First Amendment as he doused Lucy's body with drops of Trumpula Vodka. His strong, unfaltering voice boomed out, his words echoing off the walls of the crypt.

"Congress shall make no law respecting an establishment of religion or prohibiting the free exercise thereof, or abridging the freedom of speech or of the press, or the right of the people peaceably to assemble and to petition the government for a redress of grievances!"

He leaned down over the coffin, and, reaching inside, grabbed Lucy's head with both hands and lifted it, placing it as neatly as possible atop her now blood-spattered body.

"Look!" he said, pointing at her teeth. Crowding around the Professor, we peered in and saw that, already in true death, Lucy's long vampire fangs had shrunk back to their normal size. We then lifted the coffin lid and slid it back into place, covering Lucy's body and committing her to her rest.

Bernie gazed proudly at us all and boomed out, "Not bad, for a bunch of rookies!" He clapped his hands together and then barked, "Now, who's up for some pizza!?!"

COUNT TRUMPULA'S TWITTER ACCOUNT

Donald J. Trumpula@RealTrumpula 30th March, 2017, 1:13 a.m.

Why does the Fake Media never ask Hairy Hillary why she never wears silver? Because she's a WEREWOLF! MASA!

JONATHAN HARKER'S DIARY

30th March, 2017 – What a terrible night it was, especially for Arthur and Mimi, as they knew and loved poor Lucy best of anyone. Still, they can take comfort now in knowing that she is truly at peace, and no longer under the spell of the Count.

Mimi went straight to bed when we got home, and by the time I got out of the shower she was deep in sleep, breathing so softly that I had to put my ear close to her sweet lips to hear her. She looked a little paler than usual. I hope what happened tonight hasn't upset her too much. I'm sure she will be fine, she's just tired and worn out from all that has happened these past weeks, and the emotional toll it has taken. I decided to sleep in the spare room, so as not to wake her with my snoring.

MIMI MURRAY'S JOURNAL

5th April, 2017 – I was exhausted after the unspeakable events in Lucy's crypt last night. Who would have thought I would ever witness such violence perpetrated against my best friend in the whole world, or that I would even take part in it? The only thing that helped me get through the ordeal was Jonathan, who kept reminding me that it wasn't

Lucy we were doing this to, but just the shell of her body, which had been taken over by the Count, that vile, blood-guzzling, demagoguing douchenozzle, and that we had to do what we did to set her free. So I keep telling myself that, that she is free now, free forever from his grotesquely short-fingered skin mittens.

We are all scattering now. Arthur must go to Oregon to be with his mother, whose health has apparently taken another turn for the worse. Poor fellow. He's been through more than anyone should have to already. Dr. Seward, meanwhile, leaves tomorrow for a conference in New Orleans, and Van Helsing goes back to New Jersey for the time being. He's promised to keep in close contact, as we plot our next move against Pumpkin Pinochet.

In the meantime I've gone back to work. It's been so long, I feel like a new employee. But everyone was so nice. And yet it feels so strange to be there without Lucy.

I haven't been sleeping well lately at all. I keep having weird dreams, which I can't quite remember when I wake up. But in the morning, it feels like I've hardly slept at all. Ugh.

7th April, 2017 – Just received word that Arthur's mother has passed away. The poor, poor man. I wish I could go to the funeral, but I haven't been feeling well myself lately. Still not sleeping well, feeling tired and run down. Jonathan, the dear, has gone to help Arthur with the arrangements. I blame Count Kumquat for all of it, and am counting the moments until we can take our revenge!

COUNT TRUMPULA'S TWITTER ACCOUNT

Donald J. Trumpula@RealTrumpula 10ᵗʰ April, 2017, 6:04 a.m.

The Trump vampire story is a total hoax, when will this taxpayer funded charade end? No vampires here! Make America Suck Again!

JONATHAN HARKER'S JOURNAL

13ᵗʰ April, 2017 – Arthur and I just arrived home from Oregon, after his mother's funeral. I got home late, almost midnight, and Mimi was already fast asleep. I went in and kissed her and she didn't even wake up! Knowing how poorly she's been sleeping lately, I decided to sleep in the other room so as not to wake her. The poor girl must be exhausted, because she slept until nearly ten a.m. In fact, she was so sound asleep that I had to shake her and say her name two or three times before she finally awoke, and when she did, she didn't even recognize me at first, just stared at me with a sort of blank terror, as if she'd been having a nightmare. I brought her some coffee and breakfast in bed, which seemed to bring her around a bit and made her smile. Later, while she was taking a shower, Dr. Seward phoned and said that he and Van Helsing wanted to come over to discuss my work with the Count in Florida. He didn't go into much detail, except to say that they wanted to know all about Carfax Abbey, the estate here in Washington which I'd helped Trumpula to purchase. Dr. Seward said that the Professor wondered if I might have any blueprints or photographs of the place, and I told him that yes, I had both, which seemed to please them quite a bit. Seward started to ask me something else, but our discussion was suddenly interrupted by a blood-curdling scream from down the hall. I ran to the bathroom and found Mimi standing before the mirror, white as a sheet, a look of sheer terror on her face. When I asked her what was the matter, she turned her head slowly to me, then pointed at her neck and said, simply, "Look!"

I moved closer, staring at what appeared to be a bite mark on the side of her throat, quite similar to Lucy's. "My God," I said, a feeling of numbness racing through my body. "Trumpula?"

She looked at me, wide-eyed and lip trembling, and nodded her head. "I thought it was just a dream," she said, her voice choking. "John, that smarmy orange fucker grabbed me by my hoo-ha!"

MIMI MURRAY'S JOURNAL

13th April, 2017 – I had meant to stay awake and wait for Jonathan to come home, but I was so exhausted I nodded off before he arrived, and I immediately began having fitful dreams again. At one point, I woke up feeling so uneasy about everything, as if something terrible were about to happen but I didn't know what. Outside I heard a dog barking, and I got up and looked out the window, but saw nothing but the darkness, and a thin cloud of orange mist that appeared to be creeping slowly across the street towards our building. It seemed almost alive, as if it had a sentience and a vitality all its own. I felt a chill come over me as I watched the mist spreading and rising, until it moved up close to our apartment, as though it were stealing up to the windows. I got frightened and crawled back into bed, pulled the covers over my head like when I was a little girl afraid of the dark. I must have fallen asleep again, because I remember dreaming about the mist. It got inside, poured in through the window seal somehow, only it was thicker now, like some sort of weird orange fog, growing thicker and thicker, until it became concentrated into a sort of swirling pillar of orange dust in the room, at the top of which I could see one bright red light shining at me like a red eye, staring. Things began to whirl through my brain just as the vaporous funnel column began to whirl in the room, and the red light seemed to divide into two, becoming two glowing red eyes at the top of the whirling column, and I thought I heard a flapping sound, like the buffeting of wings on either side of the red eyes. Suddenly the horror burst upon me that it was just like what Jonathan had described of his ordeal at Mar-a-Lago, when the Count had turned to mist and then into a bat, and of Lucy's dreams of the bat as well, which, according to the Professor, weren't dreams at all. And in my dream, then, I must have feinted (what a weenie!), because my mind suddenly dropped into a pitch darkness of nothingness. From out of that darkness came a stirring, as if the bedclothes were being pulled off of me, and then a rustling down below. There was another sound, too, a sort of mysterious shaking sound, like a salt shaker being rattled. Then I felt a fumbling at my flannel pajama bottoms, felt them being pulled down, followed by the feel of tiny fingers grabbing clumsily at my lady parts. The last conscious effort that came from my imagination was to show me a livid, orange face bending over me out of the mist, and atop the face's head was a tantalizing swirl of swooping, blond hair.

I slept 'til almost ten o'clock before Jonathan woke me up. I didn't even recognize him at first, I was so out of it. But then he brought me breakfast in bed, and coffee. What a dear! But still, all that sleep hasn't refreshed me, as I still feel terribly weak and sort of spiritless. Jonathan suggested I get up and take a shower, that that might make me feel better, so I did. After a nice, long, hot shower, I was drying myself in front of the mirror when I saw them, on my neck, right below the jugular vein: two tiny little red dots, kind of puffy and white around the edges. And I realized that my dream wasn't a dream at all, and that Trumpula really had touched me. And that's when I screamed.

DR. SEWARD'S DIARY

13th April, 2017 – I was on the phone with Harker when I heard what sounded like a scream in the background. There were a lot of sounds then, like footsteps and doors being opened, and then agitated voices. Throughout all of it I kept trying to raise Jonathan on the other end of the line, without success. Still, I stayed on the line, hoping to find out what was happening. Finally, Harker came back on the phone and told me to come at once, and to bring Van Helsing. And then he hung up. When I told all this to the Professor, he immediately made for the door. I was right behind him. We took his car, an ancient station wagon from the 1970s – one of those old Country Squires with the wood paneling on the side – and he drove us as fast as the old wagon would take us to Mimi's apartment on K Street. We announced our arrival with a ring of the doorbell, and moments later the door flew open and there stood Harker, looking as if he'd just seen Steve Bannon with a white sheet over his head.

"My God, man, what's the matter?" I asked as he motioned us inside.

"It's Mimi," he said, giving me a look that said something terrible had happened. "She's his next victim."

I exchanged heavy glances with the Professor. "What do you mean?" I asked.

He led us into the bedroom, where Mimi lay in her bed, looking quite peaked. Harker went to her, kneeling beside her, and clasped her hand. "Show them, darling," he said, and she pulled her long, brown hair away from the left side of her neck, and then turned her head, showing us the two small holes in her throat. I let out a gasp, and Van Helsing, for once, was silent, such was his concern. Jonathan pulled up two chairs for the Professor and I, and we sat, while he sat on the bed beside Mimi, holding her hand. And then the Professor said, in a very somber voice, "Tell us everything."

Jonathan proceeded to relate what had occurred, starting with Mimi's fitful dreams last night, and ending with her finding the bite marks on her neck just half an hour ago.

Mimi grasped Jonathan's hand tightly, and then looked at the Professor. Her voice was low and raspy. "I presume you'd like to know about my dream in detail," she said, letting a brief, faint smile pass across her pale but still lovely features.

"I'm afraid so," said Van Helsing.

"But my dear, are you sure…" said Jonathan, putting his arm 'round her protectively.

"It's okay," she said, bravely. "They need to know." And then, after a pause in which she was evidently ordering her thoughts, she told us the whole story without any stops or stutters or wavering whatsoever on her part, and my admiration for her only increased another hundred fold.

"So, what does this mean, Professor?" said Mimi when she'd finished, showing, finally, just the faintest glimmer of fear in her eyes. "Am I doomed to become a vampire now, like that salmon-faced fascist? Or poor Lucy?"

Van Helsing clapped his hand down hard on his knee. "Not yet!" he boomed. "And not ever, if I have anything to say about it! But we must act, and act quickly if we are to stop this monster. We cannot waste time while the daylight is here! The sun that rose on our sorrow this morning not only provides solar energy that could break our nation's dependency on fossil fuel—which 97 percent of scientists agree is the fundamental reason we are seeing climate change today—but that sun also provides us with our opportunity to defeat Trumpula! Until the sun sets tonight, the vampire must retain whatever form he has now. The Count is confined within the limitations of his earthly body by day. He cannot melt into thin air – like the Antarctic ice sheet is doing as we speak—or change into a bat or mist. And so we still have a few hours left to hunt him in his lair – at Carfax Abbey! And so, my dear Mr. Harker, I must ask you to tell me all you know about that estate which you so capably arranged for the Count to purchase while he kept you prisoner in Mar-a-Lago last month."

Harker excused himself and went to fetch his file with

all the photographs he'd taken of Carfax, the blueprints and maps of the estate and grounds. When he returned and started taking out these documents and laying them on a small table between Van Helsing and myself, my eye was immediately drawn to a photograph of Carfax, taken from the eastern edge of the property. I knew, because I had gazed upon that very view nearly every day for the past several months, from my office at the asylum.

"My God!" I exclaimed, holding up the photo. "He's my next-door neighbor!"

THE NOTES OF DONALD J. TRUMPULA AS RECORDED ON OBAMA'S SECRET WIRETAPP SURVEILLANCE SYSTEM

13th April, 2017 – Hello, Barack. It's me again, The Donald, 45th President of the United States. So, as you know, Easter weekend is coming up, and everybody's making such a big deal. It's "Jesus did this" and "Jesus did that," and "he was so great." Let me tell you something, if he was so great, why did it take him three days to get out of the cave, okay? I mean, three days? Really? If that had been me, I'd have been out of there so fast, you wouldn't believe it. Three days? With all of the problems and difficulties facing the Jews, Jesus spends three days lying around in a cave. Worse than John the Baptist. It's like I told my campaign rally the other day, even though the campaign is over, but I'm still holding rallies because all my millions and millions of fans demand it. I told them, "I don't have time to be laying around in a cave. I'm going to be working for you. I love caves. I love laying around, I think it's one of the greats, but I don't have time. Jesus spends more time in a cave than Yogi Bear in hibernation season. He spends more time lying down than a guy on the professional luge tour. I would not be a messiah that took vacations. I would rarely leave the church because there's so much work to be done. I would not be a messiah that takes time off. Jesus is no hero. He's a hero because he was crucified. I like people who weren't nailed to a cross, okay?

He was no great leader, Jesus. Don't forget, his family went to Egypt illegally! They crossed the border! They were refugees. Illegals. Illegal immigrants. And you know what kind of people are illegals? Bad hombres. Rapists and murderers. And some, I assume, are good people. And let's not even talk about the whole episode in the courtyard, with the expelling of the merchants from the temple. That's called socialism, people! Very, very anti-business. He's turning over tables, taking their money. What's that? Bad for business. I'd be the pro-business messiah. The opposite of this guy. And his so-called miracles? He changes water into wine, okay? Big deal. What about the non-alcoholics? What about the people who liked the water? Did he ask them? Not everyone wants wine, believe me. And he's going around raising dead people. Who does that? He's raising two, three, four people from the dead? Like, zombies. So, let me get this straight. Jesus can raise anybody from the dead he wants to, right? I mean, if he can raise this guy, he can raise that guy, he can raise anybody, okay? So, why didn't he just raise a whole army to fight the Romans? He could have had a whole zombie army, many, many zombies, the Romans wouldn't have had a chance. Dumb. Very, very bad judgment. Not a good leader.

And who was Jesus' most trusted adviser? Judas. Total Benedict Arnold. Yuge traitor. The biggest traitor in the history of traitors, okay? Such a bigly traitor. The whole time Jesus is sitting down, breaking bread, talking strategy with this guy, and he's stabbing Jesus in the back. Complete disaster. I call that bad judgment. And Jesus was so outplayed by Pilate. Totally outplayed. Nobody can believe how stupid Jesus was.

And on health care. Jesus is going around healing the sick. But he's not healing the best. He's healing people with all kinds of disabilities, the lame, the blind. Lepers. People with preconditions. And for what? Zippo. They didn't pay a dime. And he didn't bother to vet any of these people. Jesus is going around healing everybody, no vetting. These people could have been terrorists. ISIS. Illegals. And he's just giving away free health care to these people. That's the disaster that is Jesuscare. It destroyed their country. It destroyed their economy, their businesses, their small business and their big business. Jesuscare was a total disaster. It imploded, and then it exploded.

Anyway, I've got things to do. I've been moving very, very heavily on this new girl, Mimi. She's the one who reminds me of my true love, my soul mate, what's her name. Looks so much like her, it's incredible. I grabbed her by Mrs. Fubbs' parlor – which is what we used to call it back in the day—and just kissed. I put my teeth on her neck but I just nibbled. I didn't suck out much blood. I want to make her my new slave/bride, not kill her. So I moved on her like a bitch, but I've been very, very careful. And now she's almost mine, I can feel it. I'm going to head over to my little hideaway now, Carfax Abbey, and get it ready for her. Together we'll make America suck again!

JONATHAN HARKER'S DIARY

13th April, 2017 – Talk about coincidence! It turns out that the country estate I'd helped Trumpula buy – which Dr. Seward says has been vacant for as long as anyone can remember – is directly adjacent to the asylum where the doctor works!

The Professor pointed his finger at me and began jabbing it at the air, as if dialing a number on an invisible phone. "But it is no coincidence, Mr. Harker! Don't you see, the monster has planned this all from the very beginning! At Mar-a-Lago he told you that he'd seen a girl – a young and beautiful librarian – in Washington. Then he insisted that your firm send you alone out of everyone at the company to make this deal to buy a property that just happens to be right next to Dr. Seward's asylum, the Doctor being a dear friend to our poor departed Lucy? And Harker engaged to Mimi, Lucy's best friend? Both of whom are librarians, and both of whom have now become his victims? And then he has his minion, Seanfield, committed to that same asylum of Dr. Seward's, where he can influence events and pass information to the Count about our comings and goings? No, this is no coincidence, my friends. This is an evil, diabolical mind at work, one who will stop at nothing to attain his nefarious goal!"

"And what goal is that, Professor?" whispered Mimi from her bed.

Bernie put his arm down, folding his hands in front of him. "I think it's clear that Trumpula's goal is you, Mimi," he said, staring straight at her. "We assumed, when he attacked poor Lucy, that she was his target, which seemed logical, given that she was a librarian too, but I think now it was always you. Otherwise, why would he be stalking you now, when he knows that we are onto him? Why would he take that risk, if he had already attained his goal in Lucy?"

I cleared my throat, and, spoke softly, acutely aware that Mimi, lying beside me on the bed, was now at her most vulnerable. "I remember something he said to me, Professor, at Mar-a-Lago. Something about the fact that this girl he'd seen in Washington who had made such an impression on him reminded him of someone he used to know a long time ago. Yes, I remember now. 'A perfect twin,' he called her. And when I said what a coincidence it was that my fiancée also worked as a Librarian in downtown D.C., the oddest little smirk formed across his mouth. It still chills me now to think about it." I looked at Mimi and saw she was staring at me, as the realization that Trumpula had been stalking her for some time now began to dawn upon her. I reached across the table and grabbed her hand, and she clung to it as if it were a life raft.

Van Helsing picked carefully through the papers and photos before him on the table, staring at them one by one. Finally, Dr. Seward asked, "Look here, Professor, what is it exactly that you are looking for?"

Bernie peered at him over the blueprint he was holding. "Well…" he started.

"I can answer that for you, Doctor," interrupted Mimi, her voice quavering. "He's looking for a hiding place. For the place where that barbecued bloodsucker has stashed his coffin. Right, Professor?"

Bernie set the blueprint down on the table and smiled widely, pointing at her. "That's correct! I gotta hand it to you, Harker, that's one smart cookie you got there!"

I said, "But why do you think his coffin's at Carfax? It could be..."

"Go on," said the Professor. "Where? The White House? That's the only other residence he's got in the area, that we know of. Unless you count his hotels. But do you honestly believe that the President of the United States, who happens to be a secret vampire, is going to store his coffin in the White House? I don't think so. Too public. Too many people. Same thing with his hotels. No, unless he's purchased some other private property, this is the place!" He jabbed violently at the blueprint with his index finger. He then lifted the diagram of the estate and shook his head. "But this mansion is huge! Enormous! There must be, what, 40, 50 rooms in this place?"

"53," I said.

"Plus," Bernie continued, "just think of all the hidden spaces in a place like that. Crawl spaces and sub-rooms and hidden passageways. We could spend weeks searching for Trumpula's coffin in such a humongous building." He stood up with a photo of the Carfax mansion in his hand and began pacing back and forth across the room, wearing a trail in the carpet. Finally he stopped and looked at us, his eyes bulging, hair sticking up wild on one side, and he lifted the photo in the air, waving it back and forth. He looked like a character in a movie, the crazy neighbor whose arch enemy is a woodchuck.

"My friends," he shouted, "I have wonderful news! An analysis of 60 million rooftops in this country showed that as much as 79 percent of them are viable for solar power. And I believe that this mansion is one of them!"

We stared at him, dumbfounded.

"Okaaaay," said Mimi. "But what does that have to do with us driving a stake through Trumpula's shriveled orange heart?"

"Don't worry, Mimi," he said, smiling broadly. "I have a plan to do just that! Just as I have a plan to provide single payer health insurance to all Americans and save our country trillions of dollars in the process!" He looked at me. "Harker, call Mr. Holmwood, and have him meet us at Dr. Seward's loony bin."

Dr. Seward looked perplexed. "The asylum? Why there?"

"Because, Jack," barked Bernie. "We're going to let your patient Seanfield escape!"

DR. SEWARD'S DIARY

13th April, 2017 – Harker phoned Holmwood and told him to get to the asylum as quick as he could, while the Professor began decorating Mimi's room with protective newspapers, hanging them on the windows and covering her bed, much as he had done to poor Lucy's room. Mimi frowned and pushed back her covers, trying to climb out of bed.

"Woah," said Jonathan, gently pushing her back into bed. "Where do you think you're going?"

Sparks of anger flashed across her dark eyes. "I'm going with you!" she said, pushing his hands away. "I want to finish this!"

Jonathan looked helplessly at me as Mimi rose from her bed on wobbly legs. "Doctor, tell her. She's too weak."

"He's right, Mimi," I said. "You've lost a lot of blood. You need to stay here and rest."

"I'm going," said Mimi through gritted teeth. "End of story."

"No, Mimi, you're not." It was the Professor.

"The hell I'm not," said Mimi, as she slowly put her coat on over her pajamas. "I'm fine. I'll be perfectly fine, once I get moving…" She tried to fasten the buttons on her coat with shaky fingers.

"I'm sure you will," said Van Helsing. "But you are in Trumpula's thrall now. In his presence, your mind will be under his command. He will pit you against us. The danger is not just to you, Mimi, but to all of us, and none more than Jonathan. You cannot go with us, Mimi, I'm sorry. I cannot allow it. Please…"

The realization that he was right dawned across Mimi's face. She let her arms drop to her sides, shoulders slumping. Jonathan removed her coat, then led her back to her bed and tucked her in, while Van Helsing rolled the front section of *The Washington Post* into a sort of necklace and placed it around Mimi's neck. "Don't remove this," he said. "No matter what. And take this --" he handed her one of his Rosie O'Donnell Barbie dolls – "and keep it close, just in case."

Mimi took the little doll, clutching it tightly to her breast. Her face got some color then, as tears began rolling down her cheeks. "Damn it!" she said, her hands balled into fists at her sides.

Harker leaned over and kissed her. When he stood, he looked worriedly at Mimi, but Bernie placed a comforting hand on his shoulder. "Don't worry, my boy. As long as it's daytime, Trumpula can't harm her. Now, let's get this show on the road. There is much work to be done!"

Mimi smiled bravely at Harker. "Don't worry about me, Johnny," she said. "I'll be fine. Go get that orange fucker and send him back to Loompaland!"

The three of us went out and got into Van Helsing's Country Squire station wagon, and the Professor stamped on the sandal-shaped gas pedal and drove us like a bat out of hell to the asylum. On the way he explained his plan.

"Okay, here it is in a nutshell," he said, waving his right hand around like half a windmill, while he steered erratically with the left. "Jack has a patient named Seanfield, who, I believe, is also in thrall to Trumpula. The Count visits him and feeds him bugs and other small creatures, and in exchange, Seanfield performs certain tasks for him. It's a quid-pro-quo type arrangement, if you will, much like the disastrous Citizens United decision, which allows corporations and the top 1 percent to give vast amounts of undisclosed cash to politicians in exchange for access and influence, resulting in a complete subversion of our political system and creating what is essentially an oligarchy in our nation today."

Harker piped up from the back seat. "But you said something about letting this patient escape? Why?"

"Yes," I said, turning to the Professor from my shotgun

seat. "You aren't serious about releasing Seanfield, are you, old boy?"

Bernie careened over a lane without bothering to look behind him, narrowly missing a small compact car, which swerved quickly out of the way, the driver honking furiously. "Yes, Jack, I am serious, and I'll tell you why." Bernie grabbed the photo of Carfax Abbey from his lap and waved it around for us to see. "As I said, this mansion is huge. Now, we can waste a lot of valuable time – which we don't have—searching for Trumpula's coffin, or we could let your patient lead us right to it. Which, I believe, he will do, given the opportunity."

I shook my head. "I'm afraid, Professor, that releasing Mr. Seanfield is out of the question. He is simply too dangerous a person to be roaming about free."

Van Helsing turned nearly all the way to his right to face me, completely ignoring the road ahead. "I beg to differ, Jack," he said, poking the air with his finger. "There is no question of what Mr. Seanfield's destination will be. We know exactly where he will go as soon as he is free. Straight to Carfax Abbey…"

Horns were honking all around us as we were now driving in the wrong lane, scattering oncoming traffic. In the backseat, Jonathan pointed at the windshield and shouted for the Professor to pull over.

"… and we will stay close enough to prevent him from doing any harm whatsoever…"

"Professor, please! I beg you to watch the road!" I pleaded, pointing toward the windshield as we nearly flattened a flock of bicyclists.

Bernie smiled. "Then you agree? We let him escape?"

"Yes! Yes!" I screamed. "I agree! Now will you pull over and let me drive, for pity's sake?"

The Professor turned back to face the road. "Why would I do that, Jack? I enjoy driving!"

Forty minutes later, Bernie and I were outside Seanfield's padded room, watching him "broadcast" his "radio show," meaning he sat on his cot in his underpants and spoke into his moldy pickle as if it were a microphone.

"Tonight's topic: should we arm pastors in the wake of the Charleston mass shooting, which was definitely not racially motivated, right, Michelle Obama?"

He then thrust his pickle at his pillow, on which he'd drawn two eyes, a nose, a mouth, and some hair. It also appeared he'd attempted to color the "face" of the pillow with magic marker, to make it appear black. He sat there, staring intently at the pillow for the next 30 seconds, before suddenly moving the pickle away from the pillow and back in front of his own mouth.

"Excuse me, excuse me, excuse me, excuse me! I get to ask the questions on the program, you dumb idiot!" he blared. "But, I have to say, Mrs. Obama, you bring up a good point. Last week I said that your husband, the gigantic racist jackass Barack Hussein Obummer, had been present on the grassy knoll when JFK was shot and MAY have pulled the trigger on the fatal head shot. As you correctly pointed out, Michelle, your husband was only two years old at the time, and PROBABLY couldn't have managed to pull the trigger of a high-powered rifle, let alone hit a moving target some distance away. I humbly apologize. Live radio."

We listened as Seanfield went to a "commercial break," which consisted of the lunatic voicing fawning "advertisements" for Trumpula Steaks, Trumpula University, and Ivanka Trumpula dresses. The Professor and I then conferred with all of the attendants and orderlies on duty that afternoon, laying out our plan for them in great detail. When all was set, Bernie and I went outside with three white-uniformed orderlies and hid behind some shrubbery beneath Seanfield's first-floor window in the back of the asylum. We remained there, silent, waiting for the workmen I'd called in to "repair" Seanfield's window. In the middle of their "repair job," they were to leave Seanfield alone long enough for him to climb out the window. That was the plan, anyway. I was gambling on the belief that, as soon as he was afforded the chance to escape, Seanfield would take it. And when he did, we would be ready to follow him wherever he might lead us. Hopefully that place would be straight to Count Trumpula's coffin. Harker and Holmwood, meanwhile, were hiding on the other side of the five-foot wall that separated the asylum's grounds from those of Carfax Abbey, so that, should my patient go over the wall as we suspected he would, there would be no chance of losing him.

Sure enough, a few moments later, we saw Seanfield's skinny, white legs appear, snaking out of the window, followed by the rest of him, still dressed only in his tighty-whiteys. As it was only a few feet from his window to the ground, he landed on his feet, unhurt, then dashed off in a straight line for the wall. Van Helsing and I followed – the Professor hauling his heavy vampire kit—along with the three orderlies, moving quickly through a belt of trees that lined the grounds behind the asylum. When Seanfield scaled the wall and went over the top, disappearing into the

Carfax side, we broke out of the treeline and ran straight out for the wall. We knew that our three cohorts on the other side would pursue my patient and make sure he didn't run off.

By the time we made it over the wall, Seanfield had already crossed two-thirds of the swampy grounds of Carfax and was nearing the deserted mansion. I could see Harker and Holmwood keeping pace through the jungle of overgrown swampgrass on the edge of the Carfax acreage. And then Seanfield suddenly veered off and ran behind the angle of the house to the left, disappearing from our view. When we got there, we found him pressed against the old, iron-bound oak door of an ancient chapel, which was attached to the house, and locked with a rusty, old padlock. My patient was talking, as if there were someone on the other side of the door, whilst Harker, and Holmwood stood quietly watching from a short distance behind him. As we crept closer, I could make out what Seanfield was saying.

"I am here to do your bidding, Master. I am your slave, and you will reward me, for I have been faithful. I worship you, Master! I defend you, always! I lick your boots, Master! Now that you are near, I await your commands. You will not pass me by, will you Master, in your distribution of good things?"

We watched him a few moments longer, and then I signaled the orderlies, and they converged on the poor man. I've never seen a lunatic in such a paroxysm of rage! Seanfield fought like a tiger, and, in fact, he seemed more wild beast than man. But the orderlies were finally able to subdue him and place him in a straitjacket. As they led him back to the asylum, he continued crying out to his "Master" until he was out of earshot.

JONATHAN HARKER'S DIARY

13th April, 2017 – Once the orderlies had taken the poor wretch, Seanfield, away in a straitjacket, the Professor turned to us and spoke. "My friends," he said, waving his arms around like a conductor on crack, "vampires do exist. And I'm not just talking about the greedy millionaires and billionaires, those Wall Street fat cats who have gorged at the jugular veins of the poor and the middle class in this country for far too long, or their minions in congress who attempt to inflict savage cuts to the throats of Medicare, Medicaid, and Social Security, all in the service of their corporate masters. No, what I'm talking about here is a real, live vampire. A bloodsucking fiend from beyond the grave. And he is extremely dangerous, my friends, for he is also the President of the United States. Never forget that fact. He has the power of the entire government at his beck and call. He commands the army, the navy, and the air force. He can also change into a bat, and fly away! He controls the vermin, the rat, the fly, and the spider. He commands the brain-dead. He can appear as mist, as vapor, as fog, and vanish at will. Now, all these things Trumpula can do… but he is not 100 percent free. Contrary to what you may have heard about these foul creatures, the wampyr can move about during the day, but he does not have his strength. At some point each day he must rest in his coffin, and sleep in the ancestral dirt of his homeland. It is here that we must find Trumpula and destroy him utterly. But we are putting ourselves at terrible risk. We gotta be tough, not stupid, so I ask that each of you do all you can to protect yourselves and each other from this foul creature. Keep this at the ready" – as he spoke he handed each of us one of the Rosie O'Donnell dolls – "and put these 'round your necks" – here he handed us each some newspaper rolled into a wreath – "and take these flashlights for visibility" – and to each of us he gave the same flashlights we had used at Lucy's crypt. "And now, Mr. Harker, do you have the keys?"

I placed the roll of newspaper around my neck and stepped forward to the chapel door, fumbling with the enormous keychain I'd taken from the Carfax file. I tried one or two ancient-looking skeleton keys before finally the rusty old padlock clicked open. We pressed on the door, and the corroded hinges creaked and gave way, and the door opened slowly into the chapel. I stood back and let the Professor step first through the doorway. As he did, he coughed, and I could see him fanning the air in front of his face.

Dr. Seward was next through the door, and he immediately let out a gasp. "My God!" he croaked. "What's that smell?"

Arthur and I entered the chapel together, Holmwood immediately covering his mouth with his hand. I recognized the smell immediately. It was the same nauseating odor I'd encountered at Trumpula's Palace at Mar-a-Lago, in the secret chamber where the Count kept his coffin/tanning bed. It was an earthy smell, combined with the strong odor of death, as if something (or many things) had died there years ago and been rotting away all that time in that dark place, the stench gathering strength and becoming more awful by the day.

The light from our flashlights crossed each other and fell on all sorts of odd forms: intricate spider webs that looked as if they must belong to some giant species of arachnid from a bygone era; small, moving things in the dark that squeaked as they fled, scurrying away from our beams back into the shadows and dark corners of the chapel; and the dust, which was everywhere, so thick it kicked up into small whirls as we passed into the room. On the floor it felt like it was inches deep, and the walls were fluffy and heavily caked with it. Finally, as we moved forward, parting the spider webs with our hands, our flashlight beams fell upon a large, golden box, tucked back into a dim corner of the chapel. As we crept closer, I could see it was the same tanning bed/coffin I'd found the Count in at Mar-a-Lago!

Muttering to himself, Van Helsing took a boombox from his kit and handed it to me. Then, pulling a CD from the kit, he put it in the boombox and told me, "As soon as I open the lid, Mr. Harker, hit Play. The rest of you, prepare yourselves!" The Professor walked to the head of the coffin and put his hands on the lid. He then looked over at me and nodded, then threw open the lid of the coffin/bed, thrusting his miniature Rosie O'Donnell doll at the inside of the darkened tanning bed, while I punched the Play button on the boombox, sending a bouncy, synthesized jingling mix of electronic keyboards, bells, and guitar jangling throughout the musty chapel, followed by Cher's deep, throaty voice as she belted out her early '70s hit, "Gypsies, Tramps and Thieves." It was all for nothing, however. The coffin was empty, except for a thick layer of ancient, musty earth inside.

Bernie signaled me to turn the music off, and when I did, a deathly silence dropped over the gloomy chapel. Bernie turned his attention to the inside of the Count's tanning coffin. "Damn!" he cursed.

We all crowded around the open coffin, then, running our hands along the rows of fluorescent bulbs on the inside of the coffin's lid.

"What in the bloody hell is this thing?" asked Dr. Seward. "It looks like a cross between a coffin and a solarium."

"That's precisely what it is," said the Professor, pointing at a built-in shelf on the inside wall of the coffin cooker, where the Count had arranged an assortment of lotions, tanning oils and bronzers. "Trumpula's killing two birds with one stone." Van Helsing took one of the corn tortillas from his kit and, breaking it into three pieces, placed the pieces inside the coffin. Then he stood, holding forth a pocket edition of the U.S. Constitution, and, raising a small vial filled with Trump Vodka, he began dousing the inside of the coffin with that failed beverage with little flicks of his wrist, while, at the same time, reciting in a loud, booming voice from the 14th Amendment:

"All persons born or naturalized in the United States, and subject to the jurisdiction thereof, are citizens of the United States and of the State wherein they reside. No State shall make or endorse any law which shall abridge the privileges or immunities of citizens of the United States; nor shall any State deprive any person of life, liberty, or property, without due process of law; nor deny to any person within its jurisdiction the equal protection of the laws."

When the Professor was finished, we went around the

dusty chapel placing newspaper pages everywhere, taping them to the walls and covering the ground surrounding Trumpula's coffin, and even stuffing the inside of the tanning bed. Then Van Helsing packed up his kit, and we made our way outside. Once everyone was out, I secured the padlock with the old key.

Dr. Seward smiled widely, hitching up his pants. "Well, that went quite well, don't you think, Professor?"

Bernie cast his gaze upwards to the darkening sky. "I'm sorry, Jack, I'm afraid I cannot share your enthusiasm. Was Trumpula at home? No, he was not. While it's true that we have ruined his resting place here, wild work remains to be done. We must go inside the mansion now, and wait the vampire's arrival while there is still light to the day." He glanced at his watch. "Twenty minutes before four," he said. "We've got about two hours of sunlight." He began walking around the mansion to the street-side of the building, where the front door was, with the rest of us following. We climbed up the steps of a large, crumbling front porch, which, like the rest of the house seemed to be in great disrepair, and I took out the rusty old keyring. I picked one that I thought might be the right key, probed the lock with it, fumbled around for a bit, then tried a second. And then a third. All at once the door opened with a slight push, and the four of us entered the dark hall.

"It doesn't smell much better up here, does it?" said Dr. Seward, crinkling his nose. I had to agree – it did smell vile, like something had crawled up there and died.

I flipped a lightswitch, but nothing came on. All of the musty, moth-eaten curtains were closed, leaving just dim light in the place after we'd closed the door, so we turned

on our flashlights and moved to explore the house. We kept
together in case of attack, for we still weren't certain that
Trumpula was not inside the mansion. In the dining room,
at the back of the hall, thick with flies, we found twelve great
boxes filled with a thick, greenish goo. "That's the guano I
told you about," I said. "He has some deal in place to sell it
to the Russians."

"Interesting," said Van Helsing, sticking a finger into
the goo and smelling it. He made a face and then wiped it
off on the wood of the box.

We found many more of the guano boxes in the living
room, ballroom, and library, stacked high along the walls
and covering nearly every inch of the rooms. There must
have been more than a hundred in total. Flies buzzed
everywhere about the place, crawled along the walls and
windows and on top of the guano chests, filling the rooms
with a symphony of buzzing. It was pretty evident that the
Count was not presently in the house, so we split up and
did a quick, cursory search of the mansion from basement
to attic, finally reconvening in the parlor, which was just
off the great hall, near the front door. There we found Van
Helsing had opened up his kit, taken out his various tools,
and set up his boombox. I checked the clock on my phone.
It was nearly five. Just a little more than half an hour of
daylight left.

Suddenly Van Helsing held up a hand, and we all held
our breaths, listening. A moment later came the sound of a
key softly inserted in the lock of the front door. Without a
word, the Professor signaled to the rest of us, directing where
he wished us to station ourselves. Van Helsing and Dr.
Seward were just behind the door, so that when it opened,

they could guard it, and cut the Count off from escape. Arthur and myself he placed across the room, just behind the mantle of a large fireplace, so we'd be out of view when the Count entered the parlor. We waited in our places in suspense that made the seconds pass with nightmarish slowness, listening as the front door opened with a groan, then closed, and then not one, but two sets of footsteps moved slowly along the hall! A look of concern came across the Professor's face – he had been counting on Trumpula being alone. And then that voice that I knew so well from my terrible time at Mar-a-Lago, a voice that we all knew at once, as there was no mistaking it, came oozing down the hall toward us. Trumpula! We all held our breath and listened as the voice drew nearer.

"I know you'll do a good job, Nunes," he was saying. "Because if you don't, you're fired."

A second voice chimed in, high-pitched, sniggering and subservient. "Yes, Master."

"Here, you're sweating again, Nunes. Wipe your face with this. I used this hanky to wipe my gorgeous lips at lunch. It's got some KFC on it. It was delicious, believe me. Best KFC ever. Terrific."

"Thank you, Master."

"When they ask you about Russia, Nunes, I want you talk about the leaks. No evidence that Trumpula has anything to do with vampires, blah blah blah. Are you paying attention, Nunes? Because I need you to put your big boy pants on, okay? No, you can keep the hanky, Nunes. I don't want it."

"Thank you, Master. Big boy pants."

"You're not very bright, are you Nunes? Not the sharpest

knife in the drawer. But you're loyal, okay, which I like, believe me. I can use loyal. Here, here's a bug. Nice, big juicy cockroach."

"Thank you, Master." He made a disgusting slurping sound.

Trumpula's voice continued. "The real story is the leaks. And Obama. Blame Obama. Always blame Obama. Or Hillary's emails. The leaks are real but the news is fake. And remember, Nunes, if you hear of anything, any evidence at all, I want to hear about it first, okay? Before the committee. Drop everything and you run, don't walk, run to the White House, got it? Or you're fired."

"Oh, yes, Master!"

Suddenly the door flew open and in walked Trumpula, followed by a short, dark-haired man with a face like a squashed potato. They walked a few feet into the room before we – all four of us—flicked on our flashlights and pointed them directly at Trumpula.

As the Count saw us, a horrible snarl passed over his orange face, revealing his long and pointed eye teeth, and he raised his cape over the lower part of his orange face, showing us only his red eyes, burning with hatred. "Who the hell are you people?" he snarled. "You're not the local milk people, I know that much!"

Van Helsing hit Play on his boombox and sent the dulcet tones of Cher's "Half Breed" blaring out of the contraption and reverberating off the walls of the old mansion.

Nunes covered his ears with his hands and began turning in circles, repeating, "I'm a good boy, I'm a good boy."

Van Helsing stepped forward holding the Rosie O'Donnell doll aloft at Trumpula. The vampire recoiled from Rosie, sneering. "You're attacking me with Rosie and Cher? A couple of Hillary flunkies who lost big. You put them both together and you're lucky to get a 3. But I promise not to talk about Cher's massive plastic surgeries that didn't work."

"Feel the Bern!" yelled the Professor, making a fierce and sudden slash at the Count with one of the sharpened Trumpula steaks, while still thrusting the miniature Rosie at the Count with his other hand, as Cher's voice boomed throughout the room.

The Count sprang back from Bernie's slash, just in time. A second less and the sharpened steak would have pierced his heart. That's when Arthur and I attacked from his rear, Arthur brandishing one of the corn tortillas and a rolled-up copy of *The New York Times*, while I raised a Rosie doll and a printed copy of the CBO report on Trumpulacare. As Holmwood swatted at him with the *Times*, Trumpula parried the thrust with a whirl of his cape, hissing "Fake news! Fake news!" Meanwhile, Van Helsing kept advancing with his Rosie O'Donnell doll and slashing with his Trumpula steak, shouting "Feel the Bern!" with each swing of the rotting T-bone. As Cher's *Half-Breed* continued to fill our ears, Dr. Seward marched forward sporting a Hamilton program and flicking at the Count with a vial of Trumpula vodka. A panicked look came over Trumpula's face as droplets of the vodka landed on his pumpkin-colored skin, burning him, the skin sizzling where each droplet landed. A couple of drops landed in Nunes' eye, and the sniveling toady cried out, covering the damaged orb with his hands.

"Ahh!" Nunes howled, bending at the waist and curling himself into a cowardly ball. "It burns! It burns!"

The vampire grimaced as he watched his screaming minion writhe in agony. "Don't worry, Nunes. As soon as I repeal Obamacare and replace it with something totally amazing, you can get that fixed." Then he pushed Nunes into Van Helsing and Dr. Seward, sending him flailing straight into Bernie's slashing steak, which sliced a deep cut into his forearm. Nunes let out another anguished squeal, clutching at the wound, which was now spurting blood, and collapsed to the floor in a lump of stupidity.

"Help me, Master!" he wailed.

"Sorry," said Trumpula. "Who knew health care would be so complicated?" And then with a hiss, the orange fiend ducked beneath Arthur's rolled-up newspaper, at the same time grabbing my Rosie doll with his tiny pink hand, burning his flesh, which began smoking as a disgusting sizzling sound filled the room. Trumpula screamed, holding his tiny, charbroiled hand, dashed across the room and threw himself at the window. Amid the crash and glitter of the falling glass, he tumbled onto the ground below. We ran over and saw him spring unhurt from the overgrown crabgrass surrounding the house. He looked up and snarled at us, his orange face a mask of hate and hellish rage.

"I win again, you low-class slobs! Sorry, losers and haters, but my I.Q. is one of the highest."

Leaning out of the window, Van Helsing shook his fist at the orange viper. "Lead apes in hell, foul fiend!" he yelled.

"So long, cucks!" sneered the Count. "Another victory for Trumpula!" Then, with a whirl of his cape, he disappeared into an orange mist, out of which a large bat with a tuft of blond hair on its black head suddenly appeared, flapped its wings and then flitted away over the trees.

MIMI MURRAY'S JOURNAL

13th April, 2017 – I was sick and tired of resting, and feeling weak, and feeling like a victim. I should have gone with them to Carfax Abbey. I don't care what they said. I don't care that I'm barely strong enough to get out of bed, that I feel like death in a microwave. I should have sucked it up and gone with them, stabbed Cheeto Chocula in the heart and ended this whole nightmare. Instead I napped. And Trumpula haunted my dreams again. It's as if he's inside my head, controlling my thoughts, and when I close my eyes and let sleep take me, he worms his way in. It was different this time, though. The first thing I remember seeing was the hair, swooshing towards me out of the sky in all its achy-breaky, golden chrome glory. Faster than a speeding mullet. More powerful than a bankrupt air shuttle. Able to leap tall, shady Russian loan-financed buildings with a single bound. Closer and closer it came, swirling across great distances and time to reach me, trailing long, white contrails in its wake. It was as if it were calling out my name, reaching out to me across oceans of time, stretching across the chasm of the centuries with its feathery follicles. I could not look away. I was hypnotized by its gravity-defying forward swoop, completely under the spell of the poofy, marmalade-colored man-tuft.

As I descended into the wispy depths of the comb-over, I realized I wasn't dreaming *about* the apricot ass this time, I was *with* him – or more accurately, *inside* him, inside his head—seeing things through his beady little eyes. I saw him fighting off the Professor, Dr. Seward, Arthur. And Jonathan. I saw them burn his pink little hand, and felt his pain as the Rosie doll scalded his skin. Saw the window shatter before him as he crashed through it, then watched through his eyes as he took flight over Carfax Abbey, over the trees, up and up, winging his way over Dr. Seward's asylum, and away into the darkening sky, the earth blurring beneath him as he flew.

THE NOTES OF DONALD J. TRUMPULA AS RECORDED ON OBAMA'S SECRET WIRETAPP SURVEILLANCE SYSTEM

14th April, 2017 – Hello, Barack. It's me again, The Donald, President of the United States after my great, totally amazing landslide victory.

I'm sitting here at my desk in the Oval Office in the White House, your former home, or, I don't know, maybe it still is. Maybe you never left. Maybe you're still here, hiding in the closet with a camcorder. You're a bad, sick guy, Barack.

So, here I am, on day 84, 85, whatever. I've been working hard, cleaning up all of your yuge messes which I inherited. Messes I inherited in so many ways. In the Middle East and in North Korea. Obamacare is collapsing, or exploding, I can't remember which. What's the difference? Either way it's a mess after we sabotaged it. Covering way too many people. Too expensive. Like Meals on Wheels. Where's the results? I inherited your mess with jobs, despite the statistics, you know, my statistics are even better, but they are not the real statistics because you have millions of people that can't get a job, okay? And I inherited a mess on trade. I mean, we have many, you can go up and down the ladder. But that's the story.

And now I have a very red outline of that fat slob Rosie O'Donnell burned into the palm of my perfectly normal-sized hand. I say very red, it's probably somewhere between a Plum and Jazzberry Jam, and it hurts really really really bad, almost as bad as it must have hurt Hairy Hillary when I won the election with my yuge Electoral College landslide. Those no-talent losers at my house in Carfax did this to my beautiful Goldenrod skin in a totally unprovoked attack. God only knows what they did to poor Nunes, my minion. The losers and haters keep attacking. Why? I'm a nice person. I get very good ratings. They destroyed my house, Barack. Filled it with fake news stories from the failing *New York Times* and *Washington Post*, and stuffed my coffin with corn tortillas soiled from being carried across our porous southern border in the dark, sweaty nether regions of illegals. Bad hombres. Disgusting! That's okay, I have many, many houses, believe me. Beautiful houses, the most amazing, beautiful houses, okay? Like my majestic Mar-a-Lago, which is the greatest estate in the history of estates. Even better than Versailles. The best. Everything I do is the best, Barack. Like my tremendous DJT ties and watches and cufflinks, which are no longer sold at failing Macy's. Boycott! I hope all the losers and the haters go to whitehouse.gov and buy some DJT capes today – and Success fragrance – love! I'm getting very good sales, and so is my beautiful, voluptuous daughter-bride Ivanka, whose line of luxurious made-in-China clothing is also selling quite well on whitehouse. gov after Nordstrom treated her so unfairly. Terrible! That's www.whitehouse.gov. Take a look, it's beautiful. See you in court, Nordstrom!

Meanwhile, the fake media keeps harping on Russia, and vampires. I don't know the incredibly handsome, powerful, and shirtless Putin, who's done a very brilliant job, have no deals in Russia, and the haters are going crazy – yet, Obama can make a deal with Iran, #1 in terror, no problem! I never met Putin. He said one nice thing about me. He said I was a genius, and I said thank you very much to the newspaper. I never met Putin. Except for the times I've met with him directly and indirectly, and he could not have been nicer. He sent me a present, beautiful present with a beautiful note. It said 'I love you, Donald. Signed, your BFF' – that means Best Friend Forever – 'Vlad.' The present was a lovely golden shoehorn. I use it every day to slip my perfectly buffed and pedicured Sunglow feet into my luxurious Gucci loafers, and I think about him every time I do it. I don't mean I think about him every time I do *it,* I mean the loafers. You're a sick guy, Barack, sick. I don't know Putin. I haven't had dinner with him, like I did with Comey. We didn't go hiking together. We've never gone bungee jumping. Except for that one time in Vladivostok. That was fun. And we wrestled once in Moscow. We were both shirtless. He pinned me, I have to say, although I did score a very nice half-nelson. And I got to know him very well when we were stable mates on "60 Minutes," and we did very well that night. I've never met him. I don't think I've ever met him. I think I'd know if I met him. I spoke to Putin twice. We had a very good talk, especially the second one, lasted for a pretty long period of time. Yuge. Very, very, very bigly. I don't know him. It's fake news. The news is fake, because so much of the news is fake. The leaks are the real story. Catch the leakers! But look at the way I've been treated lately. No politician in history – and I say this with great surety – has been treated worse or more unfairly. Not JFK, not overrated Abe Lincoln, not that convicted felon Nelson Mandela, not even Caesar. What they had to go through, getting stabbed, shot, or imprisoned for decades is nothing compared to how unfair I've been treated. I know it, you know it, everybody knows it.

I have to go now, Barack. I've awarded the Presidential Medal of Freedom to a most worthy recipient: me. The ceremony is in a few minutes, so I have to go get dressed to humbly bestow and accept this prestigious award, and congratulate myself for a great job, and then thank myself for congratulating me. Everyone says I deserve this really, really, really a lot. Smart people, those people.

DR. SEWARD'S DIARY

14th April, 2017 – As the sun set over the grounds at Carfax, we gathered up our tools, dropped what remained of the idiot Nunes into one of the Count's oozing boxes of guano, locked the place up and left. It was a quiet walk back through the swampy grounds of Carfax Abbey to the front of the asylum. Harker was quite anxious to get back to Mimi, as it was nearly dark and he did not want to leave her alone during those hours when the vampire was strongest. Van Helsing agreed. "You go ahead with Mr. Holmwood," he told Jonathan, "as he's got the faster car. The Doctor and I will meet you there." Jonathan shook the Professor's hand, and then he and Arthur climbed into Holmwood's fancy little sports car and off they flew, Van Helsing and I following in his Country Squire.

We arrived to find Mimi wrapped in a blanket, sitting on the sofa in the living room with Harker beside her and Holmwood in the kitchen, pouring glasses of wine. "Make mine brandy, Arthur," called Van Helsing, as we plopped down into a pair of comfortable, wingback chairs opposite the sofa. Brandy sounded brilliant to me, so I piped up, "Make that two, Arthur."

After Holmwood emerged with the drinks and took a seat beside Harker on the couch, he looked at Van Helsing and said, "So what now, Professor?"

Bernie shrugged, draining half his brandy in one gulp. "We wait," he said.

"Wait for what?" said Harker.

Bernie poked the air with his finger. "For the monster to make his move."

I took a healthy sip of brandy, and felt the effects immediately. "Bollocks!" I said. "I say we go after him, now, whilst we've got him on the run!"

Van Helsing lifted his glass. "And where do you suggest we do that, Jack? The White House?"

"Why not?" I said. "Let's finish it. Bring the orange devil to justice."

"Let's be serious, my friend," said Bernie. "There is no justice when the top one-tenth of one percent today in America owns almost as much wealth as the bottom 90 percent. And we will not find justice in Trumpula's White House. It's too heavily guarded. You've got the Secret Service, the Army, Air Force, Marines. Every branch of the bloated military industrial complex. We must be realistic. We have damaged Trumpula today. Taken away his refuge here in Washington. That means he'll have to go elsewhere for his rest. I'm guessing one of two places. Mar-a-Lago, or his castle in Manhattan, Trumpula Tower. But which one? That's the question, Jack."

"Perhaps we should split our forces?" said Holmwood. "Jonathan and I can go to Florida, while you two jet up to New York?"

Bernie shook his head. "Not a good idea, and I'll tell you why. You saw today what a force Trumpula is. And that was during the day, when he wasn't even at full strength! He'll be much stronger on his home turf, and we'll need all of us, working together, if we're going to defeat him. It would be insane and counterproductive for us to split our forces. No, Arthur, we need to stick together to have any chance of victory against the narsferatu."

I looked from Arthur to Bernie, uncertain who I agreed with. "Then, where do we go, Professor? And how do we choose?"

Van Helsing swirled his glass, gazing into the dark liqueur. "My friend," he said, "I haven't a clue."

"I do!" blurted Mimi, sitting forward suddenly.

We all looked at her, looking pale and small beneath her blanket, but her eyes sparked fiercely, and she spoke with an unflinching determination in her voice as she told us of her dream earlier that afternoon, of how she had experienced the events at Carfax Abbey through the eyes of the Count himself. It was a chilling account to listen to, but at the end of it, Mimi stood up and walked over to Van Helsing, then, reaching down, grabbed both his hands in hers. "I want you to hypnotize me, Professor. Do it now, and there's a good chance I'll see something that will tell us where that persimmon pervert's gone."

Without a word, Van Helsing motioned her to sit in a chair facing his. Removing a pocket watch from his inside pocket, he dangled it before her, swinging it slightly on its chain. Mimi's eyes swung back and forth, following the watch, as Bernie began to speak in an uncharacteristicly low voice. "In 1978, a meal that cost five dollars would cost about eleven dollars and fifteen cents today – a little over two times more. But a year's college tuition in 1978, which would have cost about $800, would today cost a student over $9000. That's an increase of eleven fold. We used to be number one in the world in terms of the percentage of people who graduated from colleges and universities. Today, we are number eleven among people 35 and under. Meanwhile, youth unemployment and under-employment is over 35 percent..."

I found my own eyes growing droopy, my lids dropping as I descended into slumber, as the Professor droned on.

"In 2007, the top one percent of all income earners in the United States made between 21.4 and 23.5 percent of all income, which is more than the entire bottom 50 percent..."

I was jolted awake by the sound of loud snoring coming from the couch, where both Harker and Holmwood had fallen asleep, Harker with his head hanging down over his chest, and Holmwood slumped over onto a pillow in the corner of the sofa, a thin line of drool dribbling down the side of his chin. Meanwhile, Mimi, sitting in front of the Professor, had closed her eyes and was sitting stock still. It was only by the gentle heaving of her bosom that I could even tell she was alive. Van Helsing gradually stopped swinging his watch then, and put it in his lap.

"Mimi," he said softly. "Where are you?"

She opened her eyes, but she seemed as if she were far away, in a sort of dream state. "I don't know," she said, her voice flat and emotionless. "It is all strange to me."

"What do you see?" asked the Professor.

"I can see nothing, except for a very bright light."

"Can you describe this light?"

"It is all around me. And it is… it is…"

"It's what?"

"Tinted. Tinted pink."

"And what do you hear?"

"Noise. Like a buzzing sound. And something else, behind the buzzing. Something louder. Mechanical."

"Something mechanical? What is it?"

She said nothing.

"Think, Mimi! What does it sound like?"

"Loud," she said.

The Professor frowned, but pressed on. "What are you doing?"

"I am very still—so still. It's like death."

Van Helsing's eyes narrowed and his forehead creased as his busy mind worked. "Anything else? What do you feel?"

There was silence for several moments, as though she were interpreting something. "Closed in."

"Closed in," repeated the Professor. "Like you're in a tight space?"

"Yes. Closed in."

"In a box?"

Another pause, and then, "No. A bed."

"Like a coffin?"

"Yes. No. Warm. Very warm bed. Hot."

Recognition dawned in the Professor's eyes. "Are you in a tanning bed?"

The answer came quick. "Oh, yes!" she said.

"Can you tell anything else about where you are, Mimi? A sound, or something you feel?"

"Vibrations, like engines."

"What kind of engines?"

"Powerful. Jet engines. Plus something else. Like... like giant wings, beating." Her voice faded away and she closed her eyes again. A few moments passed in silence before Van Helsing rose and placed his hands on Mimi's shoulders. Then, with a long sigh, she seemed to awake, looking in wonder at the Professor and then myself, and then at the couch where Harker and Holmwood still snored peacefully. "Have I been talking in my sleep?" she said.

"Yes," said Bernie.

"Well?" she asked. "Was I helpful?"

Van Helsing smiled widely. "Extremely helpful. You've told me he's in a tanning bed, on what might be a helicopter. Most likely Marine One, the President's helicopter."

Mimi stared at him, searching his face for something more. Not finding it, she nodded in resignation. "But not where he's going." She frowned. "I suck at this!"

Bernie showed her his palms. "Not true, Mimi! West Palm Beach is more than 800 miles from Washington. Too far for a helicopter. So, you see, you're actually quite good at this. By process of elimination, you told us where the demon flees. He's going to New York, to Trumpula Tower!"

COUNT TRUMPULA'S TWITTER ACCOUNT

Donald J. Trumpula@RealTrumpula 15th April, 2017, 6:22 a.m.

When will the Fake Media ask about the Dems dealings with Werewolves & why won't they allow the FBI to check their follicles at full moon?

Donald J. Trumpula@RealTrumpula 13th April, 2017, 4:04 a.m.

General Flynn was given a very, very good parking spot by Obama administration – but the Fake News seldom likes talking about that.

MIMI MURRAY'S JOURNAL

15th April, 2017 – The morning after Professor Van Helsing hypnotized me, we were all on a flight to New York. As the Professor put it, "We must chase this ghoul even if we have to follow him to the jaws of hell!"

At first they objected when I insisted on coming with them – especially Jonathan. But I stood my ground. I told them I was feeling better, which is the truth. I'm not going to run a marathon or anything, but I'm well enough, feeling stronger by the hour, and, as I explained to the boys, my ability to see through Sunburned Stalin's eyes is an asset that outweighs any dangers of my being there. Plus, I'm the only one of us – besides possibly Van Helsing – who has actual fight training. My Kung Fu skills might prove to be quite useful! (I've brought my Samurai sword along, packed away in my checked luggage). But truthfully, I don't care what they say. I'm going after Trumpula whether they like it or not. I want to be there to watch – scratch that, I want to be the one to drive a stake through his shriveled heart, cut off his orange head and stuff his lying lipless blowhole full of Mexican hard shell tortillas.

PART THREE

TRUMPULA'S CASTLE, MANHATTAN

JONATHAN HARKER'S DIARY

15th April, 2017 – It was just after noon by the time we'd landed at JFK and gathered our luggage. We took a cab to the Algonquin, where we'd booked a suite of adjoining rooms, checked in, and took the elevator up to the suite. After a short discussion about what our next move should be, we headed out to do a reconnaissance of Trumpula's castle. It was a 13-and-a-half-block walk up 5th Avenue to Trumpula Tower. At West 55th Street, we ran into what New Yorkers call "the frozen zone" – the barricaded area surrounding Trumpula Tower between West 55th and 58th Streets and Madison and Sixth Avenues, with scores of militarized police in riot gear toting automatic rifles. There was a checkpoint at East 56th and 5th, where the cops were inspecting the bags of anyone wishing to pass through. Luckily, we'd done our homework and knew about the Defcon 1-level security, so we'd left all our gear at the hotel. Still, it took us forever to maneuver through the bottleneck that was 5th Avenue, work our way through the crowd, the checkpoints, past the concrete barriers and the line of giant garbage trucks filled with sand that were parked in front of the tower, and finally get to the castle's golden doorway. The tower's lobby and atrium were still open to the public, so we were able to get inside eventually, passing through another checkpoint with its metal detectors and pat-downs, before finally entering the lobby. Inside, opposite a bank of golden elevator doors, a line of peaceful protestors sat on the white marble floor, some holding signs, some wearing tee-shirts with anti-Trumpula slogans. The five of us walked around the lobby pretending to be tourists, snapping pictures and taking mental notes on the security presence, before we took the golden escalator up to the atrium level, where we were greeted by even more security, including plenty of Secret Service agents milling around with wires dangling out of their ears.

"Crap on a hat," Mimi whispered. "We'd probably have a better chance of getting to him at the White House!"

All told, we stayed for about an hour before we rode the escalator back down to the lobby and left through the golden revolving doors. We walked back down 5th Avenue to the corner of Trumpula's tower and followed the Professor as he turned left, on East 56th Street, which was closed to all vehicles. In the middle of the block, Van Helsing pointed at another set of heavily-guarded golden doors. "This is the entrance for residents of Trumpula Tower," he said. Besides the machine-gun toting militarized police, a very tall doorman in a long, blue coat and a blue captain's hat stood in front of the revolving doors, smiling and talking to the cops. We walked slowly past, peering inside the entrance at the golden elevators that could take us to Trumpula's penthouse on the 65th floor, if we could only find a way to get inside.

"It's no use," I said, feeling glum. "The castle is impregnable."

Mimi glanced at me, a smile playing at the corners of her mouth. "Then we must have a plan," she said.

We kept walking down to the corner at Madison Avenue. Mimi wasn't paying attention, lost in thought, I suppose, probably trying to solve the puzzle of how we were going to get past all that security, when she stepped off the curb and was nearly run over by a long, black limousine that came speeding up Madison Avenue.

"Mimi, look out!" I yelled, grabbing her arm and pulling her back onto the sidewalk, out of the way, as the limo missed flattening her by mere inches.

"Nerds!" yelped Mimi, as the limo screeched to a halt in the middle of the block. The black-uniformed driver hopped out and opened the back door, and, one-by-one, out climbed a small, colorful crowd of revelers dressed in various elaborate costumes: Colonel Sanders, a Playboy bunny, a clown in a rainbow wig, the Pope, a pregnant nun, a giant bumblebee, Bigfoot. We watched them as they skipped merrily down East 56th Street towards 5th, the way we had just come, heading for Trumpula Tower's residential entrance. The doorman seemed to know them, as he jumped to the door and held it open, giving each a nod as they went past him into the lobby.

"Are you thinking what I'm thinking?" said Van Helsing, looking from Dr. Seward to Holmwood, to myself, and then to Mimi, who was frantically thumbing the buttons of her iPhone.

"What are you looking for?" I asked her.

She smiled up at me as she stepped off the curb and started crossing the street, heading down Madison Avenue toward Lower Manhattan. "A costume shop!" she called over her shoulder. "Come on!"

COUNT TRUMPULA'S TWITTER ACCOUNT

Donald J. Trumpula@RealTrumpula 16th April, 2017, 6:07 a.m.

The Vampire connection Fake News is merely an attempt to cover-up the fact that Hairy Hillary is a werewolf!

MIMI MURRAY'S JOURNAL

16th April, 2017 – Before we could go shopping for costumes, we had to figure out exactly what those costumes would be. So I led our little band of vampire slayers to Bryant Park, to the central branch of the New York Public Library. I took the steps two at a time, bounding between Patience and Fortitude, the two famous marble lions that have flanked the library steps for more than 100 years, marched through the tall, arching marble columns and went inside, with Jonathan, Arthur, Professor Van Helsing, and Dr. Seward close behind me. I led them straight to the Reference Desk, where a 30-something hipster sat looking at a computer screen. He was wearing a blue porkpie hat and a black t-shirt emblazoned with the phrase, "Librarians make Shhh happen." I peppered him with questions for 15 minutes, before leading my troupe to the computer lab, where we spent the next hour scouring various databases. When we left, I was clutching two lists: the first was a list of the best costume shops in Manhattan, complete with addresses correspondingly marked on the map, and the other an account of Trumpula's visitors since he'd taken office. The rest of the day was spent going from one costume shop to the next, until we had everything we needed for our assault on Trumpula's castle.

DR. SEWARD'S DIARY

16th April, 2017 – I must say I felt like a complete idiot in my costume. We spent quite a lot of time at the library, researching, after our initial visit to Trumpula Tower, and we'd chosen our outfits carefully, based on what we learned, and who we thought might gain access to the penthouse on the 65th floor of the tower. Mimi – in a tall beehive wig, rectangular glasses and a leather mini skirt beneath a faux leopard-skin jacket, with thigh-high, leather boots – looked surprisingly like a young Sarah Palin. Harker, meanwhile, wearing camo from head to toe, including a camouflage cowboy hat, camo shirt with the sleeves cut off, and camo army pants, was done up as the redneck pants-crapper Ted Nugent. To complete his costume, he carried an American flag-painted electric guitar. Holmwood, decked out in black tanktop and holey jeans, a fake goatee and a long, stringy blond wig that hung down out of a black porkpie hat with the brim turned up, made for a passable Kid Rock. But the Professor and I? We were both well hidden under long, white Ku Klux Klan robes and tall, pointy hoods, costumes that could pass us off as many people close to the Count:

Steve Bannon, Jeff Sessions, David Duke, Stephen Miller, Sebastian Gorka, Congressman Steve King… The list went on and on.

I could feel the limo driver's eyes boring into me as I climbed out of the long, black car in front of Trumpula Tower on Madison Avenue. Together, the five of us made our way up the sidewalk, heading for the doorman and the police surrounding the tower's East 56th Street entrance. It was just after 9 a.m., and, luckily for us, there appeared to be some sort of fracas going on in front of the Tower on 5th Avenue. Most of the police had left the residents' entrance to help their fellow officers in front of the castle, but there were still a few coppers standing by the doorway as we walked up. The tall doorman was there, too, of course, but his attention was focused on the hullabaloo up the street, until we were practically upon him. He turned and saw us approaching, and went straight for the door, holding it open for us as two police officers holding big, black machine guns looked on, but made no move to stop us or even question us. Apparently they were taking their cues from the doorman – whose golden nametag read "Ruppert"—assuming that if he knew us then we must be okay.

"Good morning Mr. Bannon!" Ruppert said to the Professor as he went through the doorway and into the lobby. I was next. I watched through the eye-slits in my pointy hood as Ruppert tipped his cap to me as I passed him on my way through the door. "Mr. Duke," he said. I nodded, walking into the lobby behind Van Helsing. As I followed Bernie into the tower, I could hear Ruppert calling out the names of the rest of our little team of commandos one at a time as they entered the building: "Governor Palin…

Mr. Nugent…. Mr. Rock." And then the door was closing behind us. It had worked! We'd made it!

We glanced at each other, trying to suppress our euphoria as we waited for the elevator to come down and whisk us up to the 65th floor, where we would do battle with the vile creature, Trumpula. Then the elevator dinged and the glittering doors slid slowly and majestically open, revealing an elevator operator in a bright, maroon uniform, complete with a matching pillbox cap strapped to his chin. On his chest was a nametag that read "Rufus." Rufus and Ruppert? What were the odds? Rufus smiled and nodded at us as we filed into the car.

"Goin' up to see Mr. Trumpula again, Mr. Bannon? Or you headin' to your apartment?" Rufus asked the Professor.

Bernie grunted from beneath his hood. "Take us to the penthouse, Rufus."

The elevator operator punched some numbers on a golden keypad next to the elevator buttons. The fulgent doors slid closed, and we began a smooth and silent ascent to the top of the castle. Half-a-minute later, the elevator glided to a stop and the gilded doors slid open. Mimi left the car first, Rufus lifting his cap slightly off his head as she passed. "Nice to see you again, Governor."

"You betcha!" she snapped, smiling and winking at him as she stepped into the gold-lined hallway leading to Trumpula's penthouse. The rest of us followed as the elevator doors closed silently behind us.

Two Secret Service agents stood facing us outside a pair of gold and diamond-encrusted doors at the end of the marble-floored hallway. Between the feet of the Secret Service agents lay a golden welcome mat bearing the

Trumpula family crest, over stenciling that read, "Welcome, some of you." The agents nodded and stepped aside as we approached, the agent on the left speaking our names in greeting.

"Mr. Bannon. Mr. Duke. Ms. Palin. Mr. Nugent. Mr. Rock."

Bernie pushed the doorbell, and a moment later the bejeweled door swung open to two more Secret Service agents, who stepped back, welcoming us inside.

The apartment was dazzling, there was so much gold. The walls glittered with 24 karats, the floor was gleaming marble. A giant, crystal chandelier hung from the entryway's mirrored ceiling. White marble columns were everywhere. It was like stepping into the Palace of Versailles, or maybe that of Saddam Hussein.

"Holy shit!" whispered Holmwood/Kid Rock. "Look at this place! Is this for real?"

Before anyone could answer, the Professor removed his pocket watch from beneath his KKK robes and turned to the two agents guarding the door. He held the swinging watch in front of their faces. "My friends," he said. "Did you realize that there is not a single state in the country out of 50 where you can afford even a tiny one-bedroom apartment working 40 hours a week on the minimum wage, according to the National Low Income Housing Coalition? Millions of people are struggling to get by on two or even three minimum wage jobs, while millionaires and billionaires suck the lifeblood out of the poor and the middle class and live like kings and queens. It is not moral, not acceptable, and not sustainable that the top one-tenth of one percent now own almost as much wealth as the bottom 90 percent, or that the top 1 percent in recent years has earned 85 percent of all new income. According to one study, the top 1 percent captured 91 percent of pre-tax, pre-transfer income from 2009 to 2012...."

I watched, amazed, as, within seconds, the two agents' eyes drooped closed and they slumped to the floor, unconscious.

"My God!" I said, staring at the Professor. "That is truly fantastic! You must teach me how to do that!"

"Later," said Bernie. He walked quickly through a pair of immense white marble columns that led to a sitting room that was not much larger than your average airplane hangar. I felt my breath catch in my throat as I entered the room behind him, and with good reason: it was spectacular. Floor-to-ceiling marble, with touches of gold everywhere. A marble fountain gurgled pleasantly behind a semi-circular ivory couch, which faced its twin across a couple of acres of brushed marble on the other side of the room. Another glittering crystal chandelier hung beneath the frescoed tableau painted on the ceiling above, depicting Apollo crossing the heavens in his chariot. On the couches lay red and royal blue pillows, emblazoned in gold with the Trumpula family crest. Cream-colored Louis XIV armchairs were placed carefully around the room in perfect symmetry, each of them worth more than the average American family earned in a year. Renoir's "La Loge" hung on one wall in an ornate golden frame. The lamps and candelabras were all gilded in gold as well, and golden cherubs adorned the side tables, while Greek vases in Athenian style sat—again in perfect symmetry—atop the mantel above a white marble fireplace. Hanging above the mantel was another portrait of blond Apollo in his chariot; this time he was being led by Aurora in a billowing, golden dress. And across the room, huge, floor-to-ceiling windows showed off a stunning view of the Manhattan skyline and Central Park, where the puny people scurried about like tiny, insignificant ants some 60 floors below.

The Professor removed his pointy hood, looked around and said, "This will do." He then slid out of his KKK robe, dropping it to the floor. On his back was his vampire kit, strapped over his shoulders like a backpack. Moving quickly, he slid the kit off his shoulders and laid it down on a gold-leafed coffee table. Unzipping the bag, he began handing us our weapons: wooden stakes and heavy, wooden mallets, little Rosie O'Donnell dolls, small vials of Trumpula vodka, rolled-up editions of various newspapers, and plastic bags filled with Mexican tortilla shells. Finally, he removed from his kit his boombox, set it on the table, and put his finger on the "Play" button. "Places, everyone!" he barked.

As Holmwood and I moved to opposite ends of the room and took up defensive postures with our weapons at the ready, Jonathan handed the neck of his Ted Nugent guitar to Mimi, and the two played a tug-of-war. The neck came off in Mimi's hands, and, reaching inside, she pulled out her gleaming Samurai sword, sharpened to a deadly edge. She and Jonathan then went back-to-back in the center of the room, and Mimi raised the blade to her shoulder in a striking pose. Slowly, she turned her head and nodded at Van Helsing. The Professor pressed "Play," and the intoxicating rhythm of Sonny and Cher's "The Beat Goes On" came pounding out of the boombox and began reverberating throughout the penthouse.

TRUMPULA

Drums keep pounding a rhythm to the brain
La de da de de, la de da de da

Within moments we heard doors opening, footsteps clapping the marble floor, rushing toward us from the recesses of the lavish apartment. Then, without a word the vampires began to appear, swooping in through the marble columns at both ends of the room, snarling and hissing, mouths open revealing gleaming white fangs. I recognized them all. Reince Priebus hurled himself at Holmwood, who blinded the pointy-headed Chief of Staff with a douse of Trumpula vodka; then, as Priebus writhed in agony on the marble floor, the Professor drove a wooden stake through his heart, yelling "Feel the Bern!"

Steve Bannon lumbered in, sneering at Jonathan, who sent him flying with rapid-fire blows from a rolled-up copy of *The New York Times*; then, as Bannon whirled back on them, Mimi snapped his smirking head back with a roundhouse kick to the chin, then lopped his bulbous topper off with her sword and sent it bouncing toward the fountain.

A swaggering Michael Flynn let out a string of expletives as he leaped at me. I simply stuck out a wooden stake and let him impale himself on it. As he squirmed on the stick, squirting invectives from his sneering mouth and blood from his gaping wound, Mimi twirled like a ballerina, swinging her sword, and sent his noggin flying onto one of the Louis XIV armchairs, completely ruining the upholstery of the expensive seat cushions.

The real Ted Nugent bounded in, covered in camouflage, waving twin AK-47s – one in each hand – and pulled the triggers, screaming.

"Unclean vermin! Subhuman mongrels!" he yelled, as the machine guns belched flame and lead, cutting a jagged, zig-zag swath of bullet holes across the marble walls. A ricochet caught me in the shoulder and I went down, but it was only a flesh wound. I watched in awe as Mimi ducked the sweep of his machine gun fire, sliding just beneath the Nuge's tattooed arms as they crisscrossed, guns spewing death just inches above her head. She rolled and in one motion sprang upright behind him, delivering a vicious dragon punch to Nugent's kidney before swinging her sword in a swift downward arc, hacking off both of the schlock rocker's arms at the elbow in one swoop. The Motor City Draft Dodger dropped to his knees, wailing like a baby with a full diaper, and then we smelled it. He'd soiled himself again, filled his pants with fear, just as he had when dodging the draft back in the '60s.

"You worthless bitch!" he howled, as he writhed on the white marble floor in his own filth, blood spurting from his empty arm sockets.

"Oh, shut up!" yelled Harker, stuffing the armless redneck vampire's mouth full of Tofu, and all the Nuge could do was mumble incoherently, eyes wide with terror and disgust as Bernie lined a stake up over the redneck's corrupted heart.

"Feel the Bern!" yelled Van Helsing, as he swung the sledge hammer, driving the stake straight through Nugent's pallid chest, just before Mimi swung the blade again and hacked his head clean off, sending it bounding across the room like a soccer ball.

Yet the vampires weren't done. They kept coming. Tough-squinting albino Mike Pence in his ill-fitting leather military jacket, Trumpula's dimwitted trophy-hunting sons, Donald Jr. and Eric, a shrieking Betsy DeVos, zombie-eyed Paul Ryan, and a chinless, turkey-necked Mitch McConnell. Gary Busey, with his giant teeth, shrieking, "I will rip out your spleen and eat it like a banana!" Stephen Miller flashing white power signs with his bony fingers, and the beat went on. We fought them off, scalded them with Trumpula's bad vodka, burned them with Rosie O'Donnell dolls, whacked them with the power of the press, staked them through their shrunken, soulless hearts, and Mimi sliced off every one of their rotten, bloodsucking heads. Their black, poisoned blood flowed like a river across Trumpula's expensive marble tiles, until finally, it was over. Van Helsing shut off the boombox, and silence descended over the penthouse like a shroud.

The five of us looked at each other, taking inventory. Other than my shoulder wound and a couple of other minor nicks here and there, we were unharmed and completely victorious. Except for one thing: there was no Trumpula. Long, silent seconds dragged by as that realization dawned upon us. Where was he?

"My friends," said Bernie, "this situation is totally unacceptable. We must find Trumpula. He has to be here somewhere. Let's spread out and conduct a search. Leave no golden ashtray unturned!"

For the next 20 minutes we searched all three floors of that gold-slathered penthouse, yet we discovered no sign of the Count.

It was Holmwood who finally discovered it, off the kitchen, a solid gold door with stone steps behind it descending into the dark.

Van Helsing clapped his hands loudly. "Aha! Down! Yes! We must go down! Always down with these creatures!" He took flashlights out of his vampire kit and handed one to each of us, then slung the kit over his shoulder and led us down that narrow, steeply winding descent.

Down those cold stairs we paraded, down and down, 60 stories down all the way to the ground, and still down, into the basement of Trumpula's golden castle. Finally, after what seemed an eternity, we came to the end of our declination: a small, arched vestibule at the bottom of the stairway that led to an ancient door, encrusted with jewels and glittering flecks of gold that formed the Trumpula family crest. Van Helsing pushed at the door, but it didn't budge, so the four of us joined him, squeezing beside him in the narrow vestibule, putting all of our shoulders into it. The door creaked and groaned like an old ghost, finally giving way, swinging inward to utter darkness. The Professor aimed his flashlight into the pitch black space beyond, and stepped inside. The rest of us followed him into the dark.

The cellar was cold and stank of rot, moldy earth, death and suntan oil. The light from our flashlights cut through the darkness to reveal that we were walking down a narrow, winding corridor made of ancient stone, with dark doorways leading off to dead ends and dingy, empty rooms. Rats and other small creatures of the dark squeaked and scurried out of our way as we moved forward. A thin mist seemed to rise from the cracks in the dirty cement floor, surround us and fill the dingy corridor, forming weird shapes in the beams of our flashlights. I became aware of a faint sound, like the soft murmur of female voices, coming from somewhere deep within that dark labyrinth. As we moved ahead, the murmuring grew louder, occasionally punctuated by the high-pitched, tittering laughter of women, echoing thinly down the musty stone walls. The laughter took on an eerie, almost musical quality. It sounded, to me, like the laughter of the damned.

"Stay together," Van Helsing barked at us over his shoulder. "Don't get separated."

The laughter continued, until eventually we came to what seemed like its source – behind an ancient doorway on our right. We crowded around the door, readying our weapons, and then the Professor grabbed the doorknob and turned. The portal opened, and we entered through it into pitch blackness. Our flashlight beams careened around like crossing sword blades, cutting through the darkness and highlighting a horde of floating dust motes that hung in the vaporous mist within. And then those same soft voices came to us from deep within the room, beyond the reach of our flashlights, female voices, whispering in another language – Russian, I thought. And there was something else. Another sound, like the light tinkling of rain, followed by the voice of a man, softly moaning, and the acrid smell of urine in the musty air.

JONATHAN HARKER'S DIARY

16th April, 2017 – I felt an icy chill tingle my spine when I heard that familiar, silvery laughter, the female voices speaking softly in Russian, and then the telltale tinkle of micturation befouling my nostrils. The abject terror I'd felt in the Count's palace at Mar-a-Lago some four months ago came rushing back to me then, like a sharp blade piercing my chest. "My God," I gasped. "The pee hookers!"

I turned my flashlight toward the sound, and the beam of light settled on a large bed on which several pale shapes wriggled and writhed. Two of those weird sisters – the blondes – roiled naked atop the pale form of what appeared to be a man, while the redhead squatted over his bare, glistening chest. They seemed completely oblivious to our presence, and continued to giggle and whisper in Russian.

It was the man, if you could call him that, who raised his head suddenly and turned toward us with a sneer on his thin lips. Revulsion pierced my marrow as I gazed at the most hideous vampire of them all, bald, pointy-eared and beady-eyed, his skin sallow as a rotten onion. He was a hook-nosed ringer for Count Orlok from the old silent film *Nosferatu*.

Suddenly one of the blondes turned her head toward us, hissing, revealing gleaming white fangs. Her face transformed into a vile, frightful evil, hateful eyes sunk deep into blackened sockets, one long, bony arm reaching out as she pointed at us. She leaped at us with a superhuman bound, letting out a high-pitched, animalistic howl. Mimi stepped forward and delivered a roundhouse kick to her face, sending several of the venomous harpy's teeth clattering to the floor like Chiclets. As blood spurted from the vampire's mouth, Mimi swung her Samurai sword and sliced her blonde, shrieking head clean from her neck, just as Van Helsing doused her body with Trumpula's vodka. Mimi gasped in horror as the headless body, steaming from the vodka and gushing blood from its withered neckhole, struggled to its feet, while the ghastly creature's malignant, disembodied head continued to hiss at us from the corner of the room, blood spilling from its lurid mouth, its sunken eyes filled with hate and rage. Holmwood then lunged forward and plunged a wooden stake into the creature's sightless, lurching torso, and the blonde let out one last wail that trailed off to silence as her hideous face and skeletal body both crumbled to dust.

And then it was the other two pee hookers hurling themselves at us in a shrieking frenzy. I swatted the blonde with *The L.A. Times*, and Van Helsing impaled her on a rotten Trumpula steak, yelling, "Feel the Bern!" She emitted a horrid screeching, clutching at the wooden spike jutting from her chest, as Arthur produced a long, curved knife and, with a flourish, sliced her blonde head from her shoulders. Meanwhile, I stabbed the redhead through the breast with one of Trumpula's cheap beefsteaks. The vampiress writhed, arms flailing, black blood spewing from her gaping wound, an otherworldly howl streaming from her blackish lips, until Mimi hacked her head off with one clean sweep of her Katana blade, and the once voluptuous beauty turned to blackened dust, joining her sisters in a heap of ash on the floor.

A soft whimper drew our attention to the hideous, bald, pointy-eared vampire cowering on the bed. Count Orlok gnashed his disgusting, sharp little teeth and let out a pathetic whine.

"Kill the vampire!" yelled Holmwood, perhaps suffering from a mild case of bloodlust. Van Helsing raised a wooden stake, poised to strike.

The nosferatu let out a pathetic gurgling sound, cowering away from us. "No, wait!" he cried in a high-pitched whine.

"I'm not a vampire! It's me, Rudy Giuliani! Mr. 9/11! America's mayor!"

The Professor lowered the stake to just above Giuliani's heart and held it there, as, with his other hand, he raised the sledgehammer.

"Your honor," he said as he swung the hammer, "feel the Bern!"

MIMI MURRAY'S JOURNAL

16th April, 2017 – It felt as if we'd dispatched scores of vampires, and yet our target still eluded us. The killing room full of Trumpula's dead pee hooker brides was silent now except for our heavy breathing. We gathered our gear and moved on, hunting the Count. The passageway grew so narrow that we had to walk single-file, and, being the last out of the room, I brought up the rear, following Jonathan, our shadows dancing on the walls in the flickering light of our flashlights. As I passed yet another darkened doorway, I thought I saw a shadow flit across the portal, and, as I paused to investigate, a fine mist seemed to creep from beneath the doorway and envelop me. I felt a sudden chill, as if icy fingers were crawling over my skin, wrapping tightly around me and pulling me towards that dark room beyond the door. It felt as if the fog were seeping through my skin, into my pores and bloodstream, clouding my thoughts and taking hold of my will. I could hear a familiar voice calling to me through the mist, calling my name, and I felt myself turning, moving slowly and silently away from Jonathan and the others, my hand quietly turning the doorknob as I opened the door and slipped inside.

I felt my fingers move over the flashlight's button and turn off the light, so that I was immersed in dark gloom now, moving slowly through the dim room. It was so dark I was unable to see anything at all; I felt like I was blind, and yet, somehow, my body knew exactly where to go, as if I were a puppet being controlled by some unseen hand. I heard that odd whispering voice again, calling my name, and I knew it was him, leading me to him. I moved as if in a trance, following the sound of his voice through the darkness, until I saw a flickering light up ahead, and then another, and another, small, softly quivering flames shimmering in the distance as if calling me ahead through the dark sweep of time. And I heard another sound now, too, like water softly sloshing in a tub. As I drew nearer and nearer to the tiny lights, I could make out four flames forming a rectangle, casting a soft glow that grew brighter and brighter. I was walking down a long hallway toward the flickering rectangle of lights. And I could see a form now, in the middle of the lights, a bright, fluffy, waving poof of what looked like cotton candy in the middle of the four points of light. Trumpula's hair! It grew larger and larger, pulling me toward it, calling my name, dragging me forward to my doom. And then I could see his face, too, the color of ripe cantaloupe beneath the tuft of swooping hair, and the sound of softly lapping water growing louder and louder. I kept moving toward him, until I was there, in the room with him, gazing down at Trumpula soaking in a solid gold bath in the center of four softly glowing candles burning on the four corners of the golden bathtub.

The Count's beady, red eyes burned brightly at me from his burnt orange face, and he grinned lasciviously beneath that ridiculous, swirly blond bird's nest atop his head. I could see his tiny, pink hands poking up from the dark bathwater at several small, toy boats floating on the surface.

"Hello, Mimi," he said, pursing his lips. "You look like a very young, less insane Sarah Palin." He gave one of the boats a little push with his little sausage fingers. "This is my very powerful armada. I have submarines, cruisers, destroyers, PT boats, and an aircraft carrier. They're all steaming toward the Korean Ocean after that little Korean gentleman threatened me. And now the time for talk is over. We're going to abandon the failed policy of strategic patience. They've been talking with this gentleman for a long time. Clinton, Obama, Hairy Hillary. They've all been outplayed by this gentleman, who's a very sharp cookie. Everyone's been outplayed."

Even in my fogged, hypnotic state, I realized how utterly insane he was. I stared at his bloated, orange face and said: "You're the one who's been outplayed, Mister Very Good-Brain."

"Fake news! Alternative facts!" yelled Trumpula, smashing his tiny fists down into the bath, splashing water everywhere and causing a mini tsunami in the tub, which sunk his boats.

"Boy," I said. "Looks like someone got up on the wrong side of the coffin this evening."

He ignored me, scrambled around in the water with his stubby carrot fingers, trying to right his little toy boats. "Look what you've done!" he pouted. "You're trying to sink my very powerful armada, just as it was steaming towards Iraq."

"You mean North Korea?" I said.

"Yes, that's right. North Crimea. Very powerful armada. I ordered it to steam towards North Crimea. I remember it very clearly. I was sitting at the table with Chairman Mao of China, we had just finished dinner…"

"President Xi," I said, shaking my head.

"What's that?"

"President Xi. That's who you had dinner with. President Xi of China. Chairman Mao died like forty years ago."

He didn't bat a fake eyelash. "Yes. We're now having dessert – and we had the most beautiful piece of chocolate cake that you've ever seen – and Chairman Shoe was enjoying it. So what happens is, I said to Shoe, 'We've just sent our very powerful armada steaming to Syria, and I wanted you to know this before you finished your extremely beautiful, adorable piece of chocolate cake, which is so amazing I want to have sex with that cake and have its little chocolate babies. Little baby chocolate cupcakes all coming out of my wherever. And Chairman Shoe was eating his cake. And he was silent."

"So you were basically flirting with nuclear war during dinner," I said. "Hmm. I'm just wondering, what type of wine goes best with radioactive fallout?"

He stood up in the tub, completely naked, water dripping off his lumpy, Oompa Loompa body. "Do me a favor, Mimi, hand me that towel, would you? I need to dry my tremendously supple Atomic Tangerine skin."

I grabbed an enormous, amazingly soft, fluffy white Egyptian cotton towel from a gold-encrusted table beside me and handed it to him. He took it and began drying himself off as I watched. I slowly crept both hands to the Katana sword hanging from my belt, my knuckles going white around the leather handle. But somehow I couldn't draw the blade. I couldn't move. All I could do was stand there like a mute statuette and watch as he finished drying his pumpkin-colored skin, then wrapped himself in a red terrycloth robe with the Trump family crest embroidered in gold across the chest. He took a package of Tic Tacs out of the pocket and shook them, then popped two into his mouth and began moving slowly toward me, smiling the unctuous, well-lubed smile of a fraudulent guano salesman.

"Now," he said, pushing his lips at me. "I'm going to move on you like a bitch, grab you by Satan's Doorbell – which is what we used to call it back in the day – and just kiss. Then we'll have sloppy, disgusting, interracial human-on-vampire sex, which may or may not include you peeing on me, and then later, I'll take you back to my amazingly opulent palace at Mar-a-Lago, where you'll become my newest bride."

God, I just wanted to punch his stupid chickenhawk marsala face. I wanted to call him a pathetic, double-dealing, flim-flamming, serial sexual assaulting, tax-dodging, dinky-fingered, daughter-lusting, racist dog-whistling, pathologically-lying, worker-chiseling, Russian bribe-taking, investor-scamming, yam-faced rube bamboozler. But somehow I couldn't. I couldn't do anything, couldn't speak, couldn't move, couldn't lift a finger to stop him as he oozed his slimy way toward me.

"I know you still feel loyalty to Harker, your fiancée, who's a pathetic loser, believe me. He'll never make America suck again! I know this is torture for you, Mimi," he said, gliding closer to me. "Not like waterboarding torture – which is so borderline, it's like your minimal, minimal, minimal torture – but more like Chinese water torture or… some other method that's used to… torture people. But it will all be over very, very quickly. Just one little bite from my amazingly sharp and beautiful teeth, and I'll make you immortal, like me. You'll become my new bride, and it'll be great. You'll have a tremendous time, believe me. So tremendous, you'll get tired of all the tremendousness. You'll say, Donald, that's enough tremendousness. If it gets any more tremendous, I'll get a headache. But I'll say, no, it'll keep being tremendous for a few more years, until you're 35, and then I'll dump you for a younger model, but until then, it'll be so great, so great, believe me." And then he reached down between my legs and I let him, cooed softly into his crinkled orange ear, just like he was surely used to, let him kiss me clumsily on the neck, let him think I was enjoying it, think that he was driving me crazy, that he was still winning, as he always thought he was. And when I felt him lift his head, raising his puckered, pink lips from my neck and open his small, sphincter-shaped mouth to reveal those sharp, gleaming white fangs, I pulled a rotten Trumpula steak out from under my incredibly sad Sarah Palin leopard-skin coat, and just as he put those teeth to my neck, I clamped my legs together tight as a sausage grinder, trapping his plump little lady-groper in my twaddle dandy—as they apparently used to call it, back in the day—and hissed, "This is for Hillary!" as I drove the rotten Trumpula T-bone through his back and straight into his equally rotten heart. Then I grabbed him by the swirly blond hair as he gasped, clutching at the pointy end of the steak bone that jutted from his chest. His red, burning eyes seethed with rage as I jerked his head up hard to look at me, but I smiled as I saw that rage turn to panic when he saw the gleaming metal of my blade as I raised it high above my head.

I felt my jaw tighten with emotion as my eyes locked on his, a surge of determination coursing through my blood as I opened my mouth to speak the words I had longed to say to the bloated orange bloodsucker.

"And this," I hissed, my knuckles whitening around the handle of the sword, my bicep muscle tensing, "is for *Lucy*!"

JONATHAN HARKER'S JOURNAL

16th April, 2017 – I don't know how long we'd been walking through that labyrinthine maze when we heard a muffled voice crying out from somewhere off in the distance ahead. We followed the sound of the voice, moving quickly through the cramped corridor until we came to a side passage that eventually opened into a large, cave-like room with a dirt floor. In the center of that dirt floor was a large, round hole, like a well, out of which rose a high-pitched voice, echoing up from the bottom.

"Help!" screamed the voice. "Get me out of here! Somebody, please! You've gotta get me out of here! He's crazy!"

We ran to the edge of the hole and looked in. There, at the bottom of a 20-foot drop, was Richard Simmons. He looked terrible, dirty, emaciated and haggard, his fuzzy, bubble-afro matted and unkempt, his clothes – a glittery gold tank top with matching gold short shorts – stained and torn. God only knew how long he'd been down there. It could have been since the '90s for all I knew. When he saw us he fell to his knees, clasped his hands together as if in prayer, and began to weep.

"Oh, thank you, Jesus!" he wailed. "Thank you, Jesus! If I had to dance my pants off one more time, well I just couldn't do it, that's all." He broke down in sobs then, tears pouring down his cheeks as he gazed up at us.

"Hang on, Richard Simmons!" Van Helsing yelled, as he took a sturdy, mountain-climbing rope out of his kit, handing one end to me. "Here, Mr. Harker," he said. "You and Arthur take this end, Mimi too, and we will pull him…" He stopped talking, mouth hanging open, a look of sudden alarm blanching his face as his eyes darted around the cave. "Jonathan!" he said, waving his arms like a crazy person. "Where the hell is Mimi?"

I felt a knot in my throat the size of a fist as I whirled around in a panic. "Oh, my God!" I said. "She's gone!"

The Professor handed the rope to Arthur. "Mr. Holmwood, you and Dr. Seward stay here and free Richard Simmons from the hole. Harker and I will go find Mimi. Come after us as soon as you can!"

I was already running for the doorway, back the way we'd come, my mind filled with terrible and terrifying thoughts. How could I have been so careless? Down that dark, dingy tunnel I ran, calling out Mimi's name, my voice echoing off the cement walls and floor. I could hear Van Helsing's heavy, flat feet slapping the cement behind me as he struggled to keep up. They grew faint as I left him behind, but I didn't care. I had only one thought – finding Mimi. It seemed I'd been running for hours, my flashlight growing dim – the batteries were dying – when I thought I heard something up ahead, the sound of soft footsteps moving my way. "Mimi!" I called out, my lungs burning. "Mimi!" A figure appeared in the darkness ahead, moving toward me. I kept running, calling her name. As I got closer, I could see that it was definitely a person, walking toward me, something round dangling at the end of one arm, hanging by what looked like a tuft of silvery rope. "Mimi!" I cried again.

"Jonathan!" she called back.

My heart swelled with relief. She broke into a run, the ball (or whatever it was) she was carrying bouncing at the end of the rope in her hand as she ran toward me. She dropped it as we came together and hugged, the ball landing on the cement with a soft thud. I squeezed her tightly, holding her, never wanting to let go as she wrapped her arms around me and put her face against mine. I stroked her tall, Palinesque beehive hair and kissed her cheek, and then our lips came together in a kiss that I never wanted to end. When it did, as she buried her face into my heaving chest and I nuzzled her neck, I realized the small, puckered bite marks were gone from her throat, vanished, as if they were never there. I looked down at the ground, at the round thing she had dropped, and realized what it was, with its crazy blond swirl of tufted hair standing straight up like a knot of rope, as she had been holding it, celestial blue eyes open and staring blankly, a look of surprise on his sagging, orange face, and I knew our long, national nightmare was finally over.

Or was it?

I watched in horror as Trumpula's Caribbean blue eyes

moved, rolling in their sockets to look up at us, his thin, bloodless lips pursed, and the disembodied head of the vampire spoke.

"Oh, very touching. Very touching. But don't think for a moment this is over. I've still got a few tricks up my sleeve, believe me. If I can find my sleeves, you'll all be in some very serious trouble, believe me. Ask me if I'm tired of winning yet. The answer is no, I'm not tired. I'm going to keep on winning. Now, where did I put my smart phone? Helloooo? I'd like to tweet now! I have some very, very important things to say. Bigly things. Yuge, amazing tweets. Many, many people will be very impressed, trust me. Where are my arms? Hello? Somebody find my body. I need my fingers to type my important, brilliant tweets. Hello? Hellloooo! Okay, if you won't find my phone or my body, then you're fired. You're all fired. Did you hear me, Harker? Fired! You can go now. Clean out your office. Why isn't anybody listening to me?"

I grabbed Mimi's hand and we began walking down that long, dark tunnel, away from Trumpula's jibbering orange head.

"This isn't over, you two!" Trumpula's head called out behind us. "Come back here! You can't leave me here with no body! I'll find you! Trumpula never dies! I claim total and complete victory! Total and complete! I demand an apology! Do you hear me, losers? An apology! I will unleash fury and fire the likes of which the world has never seen! Fury and fire! And also power, a lot of power, believe me."

His threats and insults chased us all the way down the dark corridor, until we came to the jewel-encrusted door at the end of the hallway. His voice was still echoing off the stone walls as we walked through that doorway to the other side and into the small vestibule that led to the concrete stairs that would take us up out of the dungeon and then out of this orange-tinged nightmare altogether. We began to climb toward that bright, Trumpless world above, leaving his whining voice behind us, hopefully forever.

The last thing we heard from him, perhaps the last anyone would ever hear from his thin, shriveled, lips, was a word I couldn't discern. Maybe it wasn't even a word, maybe it was just a sound, one last desperate shriek of unhinged rage let loose by the disembodied head of an angry, 400-year-old demon child. Or maybe it was another language he spoke, one I just didn't understand, although I confess I have since searched every foreign language dictionary I could find, as well as the Internet, tried dozens of different spellings and even consulted linguists schooled in lost languages long since vanished in the dim mists of time, all without satisfaction. And so what I put down now is just an approximation of the sound I heard that came shrieking after us down that dark tunnel like a banshee from hell. As to its meaning, that is anyone's guess, and perhaps we'll never know, unless somehow Trumpula's head still lives, and someone stumbles upon it in that dank dungeon we left it in. And if they do, God help us, perhaps they'll ask him what it was he meant when he spewed that last long noise into the void, a noise that had no meaning I could comprehend, then or now, but which still haunts me, even today. A noise that sounded like, "Covfefe!"

Printed in the United States
By Bookmasters